Plain Wrong

Amish Secret Widows' Society Book 9

Samantha Price

Chapter 1

The wind bloweth where it listeth, and thou hearest
the sound thereof, but canst not tell whence it cometh,
and whither it goeth:
so is every one that is born of the Spirit.
John 3:8

"Have you ever lay in bed in the morning and tried to remember a dream, but find it's just out of reach?" Still in her hospital bed, Ettie raised a stretched out hand in the air. "You lie there and when you almost remember, it's gone." Ettie coughed, and her lungs wheezed. She did her best to take a deep breath. "Although you can't recall the events of the dream, you can feel the essence." She turned her head toward her *schweschder* Elsa-May, who sat in the chair by her bed.

"Are you sure you're alright, Ettie? You're not making sense, and you shouldn't talk so much." Elsa-May stood and poured her a glass of water. "Here, have some of this."

1

Ettie dug her hands into the hard bed and pushed herself up further. After she had taken a sip of water, she handed the glass back to Elsa-May. "I'm okay. It's just that I thought I had a dream and when I woke up and tried to recall it, I knew that it wasn't a dream at all."

Elsa-May placed the glass back on the cupboard and sat down. "Should I call the doctor? I'm worried about you."

"It's not me you should be worried about; remember Judith in the next bed?"

Elsa-May half stood and peered over Ettie to the only other bed in the room. "Where is she?"

"They told her yesterday that she'd be going home today and this morning she's dead."

"*Ach*." Elsa-May trembled and took a deep breath. "At our age we expect that *Gott* could take us home at any time. You close your eyes and rest for a moment. They'll be bringing the breakfast around soon enough."

Ettie relaxed her head into the pillows. She had woken up that morning with the familiar lurch in her stomach when she realized she was still in the hospital. Her desire to leave the place grew with each passing day. *I knew I should never have come to this place,* she thought as the stench of antiseptic invaded her nostrils.

Scenes from before Judith died swirled in Ettie's head. When she woke that morning she glanced over at Judith and saw that she was still asleep. She had drawn comfort from the knowledge that her new friend Judith had the all-clear to go home. Ettie remembered Judith's smile after the doctor told her the good news of being released; hopefully, she would soon hear similar news for herself. Earlier that morning, Ettie's attention was drawn to the doorway as a nurse entered.

"Good morning, Ettie, how are you?"

It seemed silly to Ettie that people asked how she was all the time; after all she was in the hospital. "Still sick it appears otherwise I wouldn't be here."

The nurse smiled and glanced at the still sleeping Judith. Her smile turned into a frown as she moved closer. "Breakfast will be soon, Judith." With her hand on Judith's shoulder, the nurse whispered, "Judith, would you like some breakfast?"

Ettie grew concerned when she saw the nurse check Judith's pulse. When the nurse hurried from the room, Ettie's suspicions were confirmed -Judith was dead. The nurse returned with a doctor who made a thorough examination. He looked across at Ettie then whispered something to the nurse who promptly drew the curtain between the two beds blocking Ettie's view.

Minutes later, the doctor strode past Ettie's bed and out through the door. When the nurse followed, Ettie asked her, "Is she dead?"

"I'm sorry. I'm afraid so." Moving closer to her bed, the nurse stared into Ettie's face. "Can I get you anything?"

"Yes, an explanation. Judith was told she could leave the hospital this morning."

The nurse averted her eyes and hurried out of the room without providing an answer. Ettie leaned forward and seeing no one nearby she got out of bed to have a closer look at Judith. She looked peaceful as though she were asleep. Ettie pulled the sheet down and noticed a small puncture mark on her neck. It was then that Ettie remembered the nurse hovering over Judith's head in the dead of the night. From what Ettie could tell, the nurse gave Judith an injection.

In the dark it was hard to see which nurse it was. Ettie thought it unusual but had drifted back to sleep. Shaking her head, Ettie hurried back to bed. The orderlies wheeled in a bed and behind the closed curtain, Ettie heard the sounds of them lifting Judith's body onto the other bed, then they wheeled her away.

Ettie's mind drifted from the early morning events to the present moment when Elsa-May asked, "So what's all this about?"

"She died when they said she could go home. At first, I thought it was a dream, and now I know it wasn't." The more Ettie thought about it, the more she realized that it was a recollection and not a dream. "A nurse gave Judith an injection. I assumed it was something relating to her condition, but now I think about it, she never had an injection while she was here. I know because we discussed how we both disliked needles. She only had pills and her blood pressure watched."

"That is a little odd. Anything else?"

"Not yet, except for the puncture wound on her neck. I checked her quickly before they took her away."

"So someone gave her an injection?" Elsa-May asked.

"Jah."

Emma, a dear friend of Ettie and Elsa-May's, appeared in the doorway and hurried to Ettie's side. "Ettie, things seem to be rather tense amongst the staff in this ward. Is everything okay?"

"I'm fine." Ettie's voice was monotone.

Emma sat on the bed after she glanced at Elsa-May who was unusually quiet. "I've known you two long enough to know when you're keeping something from me."

Ettie glanced at Elsa-May and exhaled deeply. "The woman sharing the room with me died this

6

morning."

Emma's hand rose to rest against her lips. "That's awful, the nice lady in the next bed?"

"*Jah*, she was nice." Ettie nodded, and her eyes drifted to Judith's side of the room.

"But that's not unusual is it?" Emma asked.

Elsa-May said, "Ettie thinks that it is unusual."

Emma frowned. "What do you mean? Wasn't she ill?"

"She was here to have her blood pressure monitored. She wasn't here for any life threatening condition. That's why Ettie is so upset," Elsa-May said.

Emma looked from Elsa-May back to Ettie. "Do they know how it happened?"

"I know," Ettie replied, her jaw flexing. "I woke last night and saw a nurse give Judith an injection."

"I would imagine that happens a lot here; it is a hospital," Emma said.

Ettie shook her head. "She wasn't receiving any medication apart from pills and I know that for an absolute fact. I am certain it was the injection that caused it and that it was intended."

Emma stared at Ettie and Elsa-May for moments. "Ettie, do you realize what you are saying?" Emma shook her head. "Maybe it was simply something you were unaware of. What if she was in pain or asked for something to help her sleep?"

Ettie pursed her lips. "They would have given her a sleeping pill if she couldn't sleep, and she had no actual pain with her condition. I asked if she had any pain and she told me that sometimes her face burned, and she got dizzy when her blood pressure became too high. She never complained of any pain. I'm right, and I will stay here and find out what happened." Ettie folded her arms across her chest and looked straight ahead.

"What are you thinking?" Emma replied in a high-pitched voice. Lowering back down to just above a whisper, she continued, "If you are right, then you could be in danger."

"If I'm right, think of the others who could be in danger." Ettie pressed her lips together. "I could not live with myself if I left and others were to fall victim to whatever is going on here." Reaching out, Ettie took hold of Elsa-May's hand; she looked at her *schweschder* with pleading eyes. "I need to do this, Elsa-May. You'll let me stay in here, won't you?"

Elsa-May patted Ettie's hand. "If the doctor says you're okay to leave then you must go. They don't like people taking up the beds for no good reason."

Ettie looked up at the ceiling "Yesterday, I asked the doctor if I could go home as soon as possible. I will say I have no one to look after me at home, and I need to stay until I'm fit and well."

Meeting her sister's gaze, Elsa-May gave a soft nod of her head. "If the doctor says you can stay it'll be fine with me."

Emma said, "Did Judith have any enemies? What possible reason would someone want her dead?"

Ettie put a hand in the air and said, "I know none of that yet. I know that something is not right, I can feel it."

Emma looked between the two elderly ladies once again. "Suppose there is something wrong what could you do?"

Elsa-May leaned forward in her chair and said, "The same as we always do, Emma."

Chapter 2

For God so loved the world,
that he gave his only begotten Son,
that whosoever believeth in him should not perish,
but have everlasting life.
John 3:16

After Emma had gone home, Elsa-May left her sister to go to the cafeteria.

The doctor was doing his rounds early because he was operating mid-morning. He walked into Ettie's hospital room with two students behind him. "Morning," he said in a gruff tone. He picked up her chart and read it. "You appear to be doing much better. You still drinking plenty of fluids?"

"I am," Ettie said while trying to work out what nationality the doctor was. He wasn't American born. He had a heavy accent and every sentence he uttered seemed to end in an upward lilt. His skin was olive toned, his bushy eyebrows were dark and his nose rounded. She did not like to ask him where he was born even though she was interested to know.

He plugged his stethoscope into his ears. "I'll listen to your lungs." After listening to her lungs and tapping her on the back, he said, "Still some sounds there."

"I did say that I wanted to go home as soon as I could, but I fear my sister is too frail to look after me, and I'll have no one."

"I'd rather keep you in for now." The doctor smiled. "We nearly lost you. What you've got is serious; you're over the worst of it now, but I'd still like to keep you in." He turned around and said something to his students in a low voice before he turned back to Ettie. "You might be able to leave here in two maybe three days. We'll see. If you have no one at home to look after you, we can organize a place for you somewhere else. Alternatively, we can arrange home care. Do you have any questions for me?"

Ettie shook her head. He was not the same doctor Judith had, so it would do no good to ask questions about her.

"I'll be back to check on you tomorrow. Keep the fluids up. It would also do you good to walk around to get your lungs working."

Ettie smiled and nodded, but she had no intention of doing any such thing; she was far too tired to walk around.

Just when the doctor and his two students left, the sound of the food trolleys rattled in the corridor. The staff bowled in the room with two trays, left one on Ettie's tray table and seeing the empty bed took the other back out with them. Ettie pulled the table toward her. She always ordered scrambled eggs and bacon, but always got porridge and toast with marmalade. Porridge was Ettie's least favorite food; she was glad she had lost the taste for food since she'd fallen ill otherwise it would make the task of eating the porridge more painful.

As Ettie closed her eyes and spooned the watery porridge into her mouth, she recalled her early memories of porridge. Her *bruders* and *schweschders* all ate their porridge and were all allowed to leave the table once they finished. She sat there alone telling her parents she could not possibly eat it. Her *vadder* told her that back in the old country they often had no food for days and would have been delighted to eat porridge.

Ettie laughed as she remembered her *vadder's* face when the five-year-old Ettie offered her porridge to be sent to the old country. Not only did she still have to eat the porridge she got a whipping for her trouble. One day, she sat there 'til nearly midday mealtime before she ate the porridge. One of her *bruders* told her to put loads of brown sugar on the top and eat it quickly. Ever since then, Ettie followed his suggestion and ate her porridge quickly. Looking back, she realized that her *vadder's* harshness was because they were dreadfully poor. If she had not eaten that porridge there might not have been anything else to eat.

Back in the present moment, Ettie thought over what she wished to achieve by staying longer at the hospital. She would need to be inquisitive, but not so much that it would attract unwanted attention.

Being conversational and friendly came easily to her. She knew that she had a way of making people feel relaxed enough to tell her things.

As she swallowed the final mouthful of the tea that came with breakfast, she offered a smile to young nurse McBride who entered the room. Nurse McBride was Ettie's favorite nurse because she was always bright and happy. Ettie guessed her to be in her mid twenties. She was a small woman, with dark eyes, dark hair, and skin which Ettie considered far too pale.

"Has your sister gone home?" the nurse asked in a chirpy voice, pushing the large laundry trolley to the far side of the room.

"No, she was feeling hungry. She's gone to find some breakfast. She's in the cafeteria I expect."

Placing her teacup aside, Ettie decided now would be a good time to begin her investigation. "My sister left home in such a hurry to come see me this morning that she missed breakfast. I do wish she wouldn't worry about me so much."

"She's your sister," the nurse said with a smile.

"That's her job."

Ettie wasted no time getting to the point. "It was awful hearing about Judith this morning, wasn't it?"

"It was." The young nurse briefly took a sideways glance at Ettie then turned her attention to the sheets in the next bed. "But it's a common sight in a hospital."

"That's quite a depressing thought," Ettie said with a frown. "I know death is inevitable, but Judith hardly seemed sick at all."

"Depressing, but also true. I guess everyone who works here has their way of dealing with death. Although..." Almost as an after thought, the nurse shook her head and remained silent.

"Although?" Ettie repeated the word as a question. "Although what?"

"I don't know how anyone could deal with something like that, not properly. I have seen so many people work in this hospital who seem cold and indifferent towards the patients. At first I thought it was a normal part of the job, to stop you going crazy."

Ettie remained attentive as the nurse spoke, scrutinizing every word she said. If she knew anything about Judith, Ettie hoped she might say something useful.

The nurse continued, "But the longer I work here, the more I realize that you need to care. If you don't, then surely you cannot do your job properly."

"Balance," Ettie stated wearing a wise grin. "It's balance that you need."

"Yes, I believe so." The nurse pulled the sheets from Judith's bed and placed them in the trolley. As she was stripping off the pillowcases, she said, "I care too much that's my problem."

"Like my sister," Ettie said.

"Yes, quite right. That's why I wanted to be a nurse, but ironically it might be why I might not make a good one."

"I think you make a wonderful nurse, Nurse McBride," Ettie said, glad that the young girl was so talkative. "Surely being able to care for someone should be the most important part of your job?" Ettie kept a smile on her face as she spoke, although she still felt nervous not knowing which nurse could be the perpetrator. "When you say you care too much, you make it sound negative. You should see it as your strength, the thing that keeps you going to help those who need you."

The nurse was silent for a moment. "I suspect you could teach some people around here a thing or two with words like that, Ettie." Returning the older woman's smile, nurse McBride finished sorting through the clean bed covers ready for the next patient. When she was done, she moved closer to Ettie's bed and sat down at the end of it. "Call me Melanie. Or I shall keep calling you Mrs. Smith."

"Melanie it is then."

Letting out a sigh, the nurse appeared to study Ettie thoughtfully before she spoke again. "You're right, you know, about Judith. It was so sudden I still don't know how it happened." The young nurse looked down toward her lap as she spoke.

"When I began working in medicine I thought that I would be saving people, helping them keep their hold on life. But all I seem to be doing is drawing things out, delaying the inevitable."

Ettie felt the warmth of her own smile spread inward hearing the young girl speak. She radiated sincerity while discussing her job role. Melanie McBride could not be the nurse she was looking for, but Ettie thought she still might be able to help with information.

"Judith was just one of many patients we've lost unexpectedly. Loosing someone battling an illness is awful enough, but when it's someone here for something routine, it's heartbreaking."

"These other patients," Ettie began, keeping an unemotional tone to her voice, "How did they die? Was the manner similar to the way Judith died?"

"I couldn't say for sure. All of them were found silent in their beds come morning, and I know that their deaths were unexpected."

Ettie leaned back into her pillows; sitting straight was too much effort. Even speaking was an effort, but Ettie forced herself. "Judith's family will no doubt have a post-mortem to discover why she died."

"The other families didn't. It's not a common thing to do around here. I mean, with the deaths I just mentioned, not one of their families wanted a post-mortem." As if she realized she had said too much the nurse stood up and said, "Maybe, Judith's family will. Now, how much water have you drunk today so far? You don't want to have another drip, do you?"

"I certainly don't." Ettie was badly dehydrated when she came into the hospital and was on a drip for the first two days. "Elsa-May filled up the jug this morning."

The nurse looked at the transparent jug. "Good, you've had about two glasses today then?"

"That would be about right," Ettie said.

"And you've taken your morning tablet?"

"Yes, this morning when they brought them 'round."

"Very good. I better go." The nurse smiled at

Ettie and then left.

Giving a slight nod in response, Ettie watched the nurse walk out the door.

Feeling tired, Ettie closed her eyes and made an effort to recall all that the young nurse said, so she could piece things together. The young nurse said that there were other unexpected deaths. The families did not ask for post-mortems. Or if they had wanted one for some reason they did not get one. Might someone in the hospital have talked them out of it? Ettie tried to remember what the nurse, Melanie McBride said, but she could not stay awake.

Chapter 3

And this is the condemnation,
that light is come into the world,
and men loved darkness rather than light,
because their deeds were evil.
John 3:19

Elsa-May had taken a while to return and now that Ettie had woken from her nap, she was worried about her. She got out of bed and shuffled to the chair by the window. The sky was bright blue and tall tree branches swayed to and fro in a soft breeze. It was a glorious, sunny day, and she was stuck in the hospital determined to find out why Judith suddenly died. Her attention was taken by two crows fighting over a piece of bread on the green grass of the hospital grounds. Sighing, she said to herself, "That my days were so simple."

"*Ach.*" A voice startled Ettie. She spun around to find Maureen, one of her younger widow friends.

Maureen walked further into Ettie's hospital

room carrying two cups of tea and a white cardboard cake box. "You're still worrying about Judith I see? I've just seen Elsa-May, and she told me all about your friend." She held up the cake box. "Here, I bring sweet distractions. Eat them quick before the doctor comes and snatches them from under our noses."

Seeing Maureen's smile brought comfort to Ettie. "You gave me a start. You've seen Elsa-May then?"

"I passed her in the cafeteria. She told me what happened and said to tell you that she'll be up shortly." After Maureen gave her the tea, she spread a napkin on the windowsill and on it she placed a large custard slice.

Maureen bent down to kiss Ettie on her cheek before settling into the chair next to her with a large cream, chocolate cake decorated with strawberries slices. "Did you get any sleep at all, Ettie?" Maureen took a large bite of cake while she waited for an answer.

"I did last night, but I have no idea how I'll sleep

tonight. Sleeping with one eye open is what I'll likely do. That is, if I don't want to end up like Judith." Ettie bit into the custard slice, and although it tasted as divine as always, the urge to devour it didn't come. She rested it back on the sill while she chewed slowly as though it were raw dough. "Thanks for this," she said after she'd washed it down with a mouthful of hot tea. The mug felt comfortable between her palms, the warmth traveled up her arms and made her tingle. But not even tea could ease her mind after what happened to Judith.

"It's only tea and cake," Maureen said, still chewing the last of her mouthful. "I would like to do more, like care for you at home. I don't like you being here, now more than ever with what happened to your friend. Elsa-May said you're insisting on staying as long as possible."

"I must find out what's happening. I just had a disturbing talk with a young nurse. There's something going on; I can feel it. Anyway, you have your job; you can't look after me."

"I can take time off; it's just a part time job."

"*Jah*, and one that I know you need." Ettie reached to rest her hand on the back of Maureen's. "You can help me with something though. I've had an idea."

"What is it? I'll help if I can."

"I know." Elsa retrieved her hand and leaned forward. Lowering her voice, she said, "Now, hear me fully before you say anything."

"Okay, what is it? You have me intrigued." Maureen rested her cup on the floor by her feet. And, following Ettie's lead, she leaned closer to her. "Well?"

"What do you think about going to see our mutual friend to get information about this hospital?"

"Detective Crowley?"

Ettie nodded with a twinkle in her eye.

"What kind of information do you think he'll be able to get?" Maureen asked.

"Of that, I'm not certain. See if he can find anything about unexplained deaths here. How many unusual deaths or reports have been made against this place or against any of the staff? I don't know; anything he can tell you. Let him know what happened and of my suspicions."

"Okay. I can do that."

Ettie breathed deeply and wished the act of speaking did not wear her out so. "He'll be able to access all sorts of information." Ettie took another deep breath. "He's exactly the person we need to get to the bottom of everything."

"*Ach*, Ettie, we couldn't get him involved, could we? He's probably not allowed to investigate places like this on a whim. It most likely has to be official, don't you think? And, well, this isn't."

Ettie gave a quick, disgusted snort. "Isn't what?"

"Official. It's not official."

"Someone died." Ettie looked out the window, remembering how Judith loved to watch people feed the magnificent black crows. "How *official* does it need to be?"

"Yes, but *officially*, she died within the law. Surely there's no case for this hospital and its staff to answer. All we have are two old ladies who think a midnight injection, and a morning death could be related. No sensible representative of the law would get involved with that."

"First, please refrain from describing me and Elsa-May as old. Awful! Second, I've talked to a nurse who also thinks that something is wrong."

Maureen raised her eyebrows. "She said that?"

"As good as said that. Anyway, law enforcers should want to be involved with all possibilities of wrongdoing. It's their job, their vocation." After a pause Ettie added, "We need Crowley to investigate any complaints filed against this place. See if there's a pattern of unusual deaths or unexpected deaths; then we'll have something to back up our suspicions. Or we might find something to make the case official."

Maureen went to take another bight of cake, looked at it, and retrieved her cup of tea from the floor instead. "Well, we can try. I work today, so I'll go and see Crowley when I finish."

"Excellent; *denke,* Maureen. I was already suspicious, but even more so after my conversation with the young nurse." Ettie repeated all that the nurse had said, so Maureen could relay it to detective Crowley.

"You should have someone stay with you tonight, Ettie. Maybe someone who could stay awake all night? I'd do it, but after work I can't help but sleep solidly."

Ettie pushed her lips out and looked into the distance. "I'll see if Bailey can stay."

"*Jah*," Maureen said. "That would make me feel better."

Chapter 4

In all your ways acknowledge him,
and he will make your paths straight.
Proverbs 3:6

An older nurse came into Ettie's room and looked around. Nurse Bush was a stern, no-nonsense woman who rarely smiled.

"Can I help you?" Ettie asked due to the vague look on her face.

"I was just seeing if Mrs. Morcombe's son had been here yet."

"Judith's son?"

"Yes. He's coming to collect his mother's things. They're all in that box over there." She pointed to the far corner, by Judith's bare bed. Nurse Bush walked close to Ettie. "Do you need help washing and dressing before I go?"

Shaking her head, Ettie said, "My sister is helping me wash later."

The nurse nodded, and her face remained sullen.

Ettie thought it strange that Judith's son would be sent to the room where his mother had died. Why wouldn't they have left her things at the reception desk for him?

After the nurse left, panic churned Ettie's stomach. She shuffled around the room waiting for Judith's son to arrive. Chances were the hospital stole his mother's final years. Should she share her unsubstantiated suspicions with him, or would that be insensitive of his bereavement?

Oh wait; there might be an autopsy. It's an unexpected and sudden death; officials must need answers. Lost in her thoughts, Ettie jumped in fright when Elsa-May walked through the door. "Elsa-May, you've been gone for quite some time."

"Ettie, I told you I was going to find some breakfast. I left early this morning without eating. You know I get faint if I don't eat often." Elsa-May's eyes were drawn to the cakes and slices that Maureen had brought. "I see Maureen's been here."

"*Jah*, she said you told her what happened to

Judith. Before Maureen came, I talked to nurse McBride. Nurse McBride told me that there have been a few unexpected deaths. Anyway, Maureen is going to Detective Crowley, and she'll tell him about Judith and what nurse McBride told me." Ettie told her *schweschder* the information that nurse McBride gave her.

"*Gut.* Now, what are you doing out of bed?"

"The doctor said I should walk around a little. I need to work my lungs – get some air into them."

Once Ettie got back into bed Elsa-May sat next to her and said, "Excellent idea about Crowley. If anyone can help us it'll be he, with *Gott's* help."

A raised voice in the corridor caused the two to stop talking. They listened to the words spoken by an unfamiliar male voice. From what they overheard, Ettie knew that it was Judith's son. Ettie and Elsa-May watched him as he strode into the room.

Looking toward them both, his features softened. "Sorry for all that commotion. I did not mean to disturb you. I'm just upset about my mother. I've come to collect her belongings. Is it okay for me to come in?"

"Oh, yes. Please do. I've seen you visiting your mother, but we were never introduced. Come, come." Ettie encouraged him in, relieved, and intrigued to see what he'd been told about his mother's death. "I'm Ettie and this is my sister, Elsa-May."

Judith's son nodded hello to both ladies and crept in meekly, perhaps dreading the task ahead. "I'm Milton Morcombe."

Ettie knew that gathering a parent's possessions after their death was not an easy task.

"Every child ends up doing this at some point, I guess. It's tragic, but far less so that the other way around. I'm not disturbing you, am I? Mother talked so fondly of you when I visited here yesterday, Ettie. I hope this isn't too upsetting for you."

"Death is a part of life especially at my age; my life revolves around funerals of my friends. But yes, they're all upsetting, of course, they are. I'm sorry for your loss. I got to know your mother a little; we had many good conversations. My comfort is that all my friends have gone to their true home to be with God."

The man frowned then looked at Elsa-May in her Amish clothes and nodded. "Yes. That's right."

"One of the nurses packed her things in that box over there." Ettie pointed to the table by his mother's bed. "Ready to go."

"Oh." He looked a little disappointed. Both ladies watched as he looked in some drawers of the chest near Judith's bed. He looked up at them. "Just seeing if they missed anything. I'll be out of your way then."

Ettie wondered whether he wanted to stay a while, to feel close to his mother perhaps. "You would be doing me an honor if you sat with us and drank a cup of tea."

His face lit up. "Yes, that would be nice. I know there's tea in the visitors' room. I'll be right back."

Once he returned with their tea, he sat on his mother's bed and peered around the room, no doubt thinking about what his mother had seen leading up to her death. "I just don't understand it; she only came to the hospital to have them keep an eye on her blood pressure. We had no idea there was anything wrong with her; anything that would cause her death." His voice lowered when he continued, "I arrived to take her home today. They stopped me in the ward just as I was about to come into this room. They sent me to talk to someone; I knew then that there was something wrong."

"It must have come as a shock," Elsa-May said.

Milton hung his head in silence.

"Were you advised what the cause might have been?" Ettie asked, hoping she wasn't being too nosey.

He took a deep breath, but his shoulders were still low. "No, I guess these things happen." Appearing to have become more tired in the few minutes that had passed since his entrance, Milton moved off the bed then sat on the chair between the two beds.

Ettie had to ask, and there was no smooth lead into such a question, "Are you waiting for the autopsy, you know, before the funeral?"

"No," he replied immediately. "I don't think I want one done. It won't bring her back. I had a talk to one of the nurses, and she said that there was no value in one of those under the circumstances. And well, it wouldn't bring her back."

Ettie frowned. "Oh, but isn't it normal for unexpected deaths to be investigated?"

"Unexpected? She was just old; it happens to us all. It was unexpected in the sense that they told me she could go home, but I guess it wasn't meant to be. It was her time – and all that."

Ettie wanted to shake the poor bereaved man, but the weary look in his eyes told her not to double the weight of his loss. "When will the funeral be? I would like to pay my respects if I'm out of here by then."

"Haven't fixed a date just yet, but it'll be next week sometime. My brother lives far away, and I'll need to wait for him. I'll let you know." He finished off his tea and smiled, but Ettie noticed that it didn't reach his eyes.

"Oh good." *There's still time for the autopsy if*

I convince the police there's cause to have one. I need more evidence, Ettie thought. "I'll get my sister to take me to the funeral. If I'm not out of hospital, they might not mind me going out for an hour." *Especially if they don't know*, Ettie thought.

"She was a good mother," Milton said. "Probably the best mother anyone could ever have had." He looked up at Elsa-May and Ettie. "Do you ladies have children?"

Ettie smiled. "We have children and grandchildren. Elsa-May has great grandchildren."

Milton looked away from them and blinked back tears. "I never told her how much I appreciated everything she ever did for me."

"Sometimes things like that are understood and never need to be said. Your mother would have known what you thought of her," Elsa-May said.

Milton looked across at Elsa-May. "Do you think so?"

She nodded. "Mothers know. We know we might be taken for granted and expected to do things for them, but we know we're loved and appreciated.

No words need be exchanged."

Milton looked away. "Thank you. I hope she knew." After a moment, he rested his cup on the bedside table, grabbed the small box of his mother's belongings, and walked to the door. "It was nice talking to the two of you. And Ettie, I'm glad she shared a room with you before she passed."

"Me too, Milton."

"I hope you get well soon." Offering a weak smile at both ladies, Judith's son left the room, clutching his mother's belongings under his arm.

Chapter 5

And God shall wipe away all tears from their eyes;
and there shall be no more death, neither sorrow,
nor crying, neither shall there be any more pain:
for the former things are passed away.
Revelation 21:4

That night, Bailey stayed with Ettie. He slept the night in the chair next to the bed despite three nurses insisting visitors' time was over. Bailey said he was not a visitor, and he was going to stay.

The first thing that Ettie said on waking was, "Bailey, Maureen said she was going to talk to Crowley yesterday, and I haven't seen her. I thought Crowley would have been in to see me too."

"Will you be all right if I go and see Crowley now? Maybe Maureen hasn't been yet."

"*Jah*, you go; I'll be okay. Maureen did say she'd see him straight after work."

Ettie wrestled with herself whether she should have told Bailey anything at all. She wanted to keep

Bailey out of investigations given his breakdown after leaving the FBI. She was anxious to find out about the hospital, but hoped she would not be the next to receive a deadly injection. If there was one thing Ettie disliked it was feeling vulnerable, as she did now.

When nurse McBride came into the room, Bailey said goodbye to his aunt.

Ettie took the opportunity of being alone with Melanie McBride to do some more investigating.

"Morning, Ettie."

"Hello, Melanie."

Nurse McBride took Ettie's temperature. "Ah, that's normal." Then she checked her blood pressure. "All looks good. It's just those lungs of yours that need to clear."

"I'm feeling better, but I was lying awake all night worrying about Judith and how she died."

The nurse lowered her head and wrote some things on Ettie's chart at the end of the bed.

Ettie continued, "I mean, she seemed perfectly fine the day before, and then she was gone, just like that; here one moment and gone the next and for no good reason. That can't be normal can it, Melanie?"

The nurse stopped what she was doing and hung the chart back on the end of Ettie's bed. "Thing is, Ettie, it is normal. Or at least, sudden death isn't unusual."

"What?" Ettie's heart rate quickened. "Do you mean in general, or in this place specifically?" Ettie knew she was taking a risk probing so far.

The nurse looked over her shoulder at the door before sitting on the bed and facing Ettie. "Well, Ettie, you must realize that I shouldn't be talking about any of this, especially with a patient, so please don't repeat it. I probably said too much to you yesterday. I've mentioned to people higher up that I don't think some things are right. Nothing has been done, and if I make an official complaint, I fear my job might be in jeopardy."

Ettie nodded trying to will her heart to stop racing. "Of course."

"Well, this hospital, when compared to others

I've worked in, has a high incident rate."

"A what rate?"

"I just mean that in this hospital more people over fifty die without apparent reason, than in other hospitals."

Ettie moved uncomfortably. "But is that in people who were very ill when they arrived?"

With her voice now a whisper the nurse said, "What I'm sure is that most of them came in with ailments that were not life threatening. That's the weird thing, and that's why I'm whispering, Ettie. And it's why I can't say anything to anyone. I don't like to worry you, but if I were you, I'd find another hospital or go home."

Ettie gulped, almost wishing she hadn't begun the conversation. "Thank you for being honest with me. I won't get you into any trouble."

The nurse looked at the watch attached to her breast pocket. "Oh gee, I must get on. I have another twenty patients to see before doctor's rounds." Within minutes, she fluffed up Ettie's pillow, filled her glass with water and made sure the emergency button and the telephone were within Ettie's reach.

"Are you warm enough; do you need an extra blanket?" the nurse asked.

"No, no. You get on. I've held you up long enough. Thanks for our talk."

"No problem, Ettie. Remember..." she placed a finger over her pursed lips. "Shh."

"Just a minute," Ettie called after her. The nurse spun around. "Do you suspect anyone in particular is doing this to these people."

The nurse looked over her shoulder, and as she came closer to Ettie, she whispered, "I can tell you that it always happens on the 8 p.m. to 3 a.m. shift." With a lift of her eyebrows, she added, "Nurse Hadley is permanently on that shift – Deirdre Hadley."

Ettie stared at the young nurse for a moment before she disappeared. She had a name, Deirdre Hadley. It would have pulled more weight with Crowley if she had sent Maureen to him with a name.

* * *

45

Tired from having to work longer than she expected the day before, Maureen made her way to Crowley's office. She hoped Ettie would not be too angry with her for not going to see Crowley the previous day.

"Come in." As usual Crowley's tone impatient.

Maureen knew his curt tone was not a reflection of his current mood; it was simply the way in which he always spoke. When she walked through the door, Maureen noticed that his face lighted up.

"Maureen, it's nice to see you. Have you brought any of your cakes for me?"

Maureen laughed. "I would have, but I had a double shift yesterday, and Ettie wanted me to speak to you as soon as possible. She's still in the hospital."

"I didn't realize she was that ill. Last time I saw her she did have a bad cough."

"She's got pneumonia, and that's not all." Maureen sat in the chair opposite him. "The night before last, the lady in the next bed to her died, and Ettie thinks that it was not from natural causes."

"Go on." Crowley leaned forward.

"Ettie remembers waking in the night to see a nurse give the lady an injection. She was only in to have her blood pressure monitored. Ettie knows that she never had an injection on any of the other nights that she was in the hospital."

"Does Ettie know of any reason anyone would want the woman dead?"

Maureen shook her head. "No, but she had a talk to one of the nurses which confirmed her suspicions. The nurse said that there have been deaths that were unexplained and unexpected."

"Interesting; I'll check into it." Crowley opened the drawer of his desk and pulled out a notepad.

"Ettie was thinking that you could see if they've been any complaints against the hospital, any lawsuits filed or the likes."

"I'll look into things. I'll go and see Ettie myself later today."

"I'm worried about her; do you think she's in any danger? She was going to have Bailey stay with her last night."

Crowley nodded. "Good idea. She probably shouldn't be alone at night under the circumstances."

Maureen raised her eyebrows and repeated, "Do you think she's in danger then?"

Crowley laced his fingers together in front of him. "I couldn't say for sure."

"She won't leave. She'd rather put herself in danger to find out the truth."

"Yes, she would. She'd be keen to get to the bottom of things. Is that all you know, Maureen?"

Maureen nodded. "I'll bring cakes in next time I come."

"Can I drive you home?"

"No. I came in the buggy." Maureen rose to her feet. "Thank you, Detective."

"Before you go, can you give me that name of the patient who died?"

Maureen sat down again and was silent for a while. "No, I don't think that Ettie told me her name."

"Very good."

They were interrupted by Bailey poking his head

around the door. "Maureen you're here. I thought that was your buggy I saw outside."

"Rivers." Detective Crowley said.

Bailey came further through the doorway. "Ettie was worried that she hadn't heard from you, Crowley."

"I've just learned of it."

Maureen stood up and said to Bailey, "I had to work an unexpected double shift last night, so it was too late when I finished at twelve o'clock midnight. I've just told detective Crowley everything now."

Bailey breathed out heavily. "Well, if you've got it all in hand, I don't need to be involved. Ettie seems to be concerned about the lady in the next bed dying. I'll stay with her every night until she leaves the place."

"That's good of you, Bailey," Maureen said.

Bailey and Maureen walked out of Crowley's office together.

Chapter 6

Do not be anxious about anything, but in everything,
by prayer and petition, with thanksgiving,
present your requests to God.
Phillipians 4:6

Later that day, Crowley strolled into Ettie's hospital room with flowers and a smile. "Hello, Ettie. I hope you're feeling better."

Elsa-May had gone for a wander to stretch her legs. Ettie was just in the beginning stages of dozing off when she heard Crowley's voice. "Crowley, you came." Ettie pushed herself up further onto her pillows. "I'm much improved, thank you very much. All the better for seeing you though, I can tell you."

Her heart pounded hoping he had news. She needed his support on her theories; otherwise it would be too late to investigate Judith's death. "Would you shut the door before you sit? I don't want anyone to hear a word."

He raised his eyebrows, and the corners of his mouth twitched. He closed the door, then pulled up a chair and sat and leaned himself toward her.

"Maureen's been to see you?" Ettie asked.

"She came to visit me this morning early. Although she mentioned a few things, I'd rather hear them directly from you. If there was any truth in what she told me, you'd be a witness."

Ettie was groggy, and her head was muddled. She hoped she could explain the events clearly and concisely to Crowley. "Well, seems that Judith Morcombe came in for a routine stay, she had nothing much wrong with her. She even told me that they said she could go home and she couldn't wait to see her cats. I woke in the night and saw her getting an injection—an injection for what? The next time I open my eyes in the morning, she's dead. From what did she die? What was in that injection and who administered it? Is there any note about it on her chart? There are so many unanswered questions, Crowley; wouldn't you agree? I can't find these things out by myself, but perhaps you can."

Crowley tilted his head as one might to a child. She knew she had not spoken eloquently. The words she spoke to him were tumbled and jumbled as they spilled too quickly out of her mouth. From the stony look on his face, Ettie knew that Crowley did not think there was anything suspicious in what had happened. It was all too easy to forget that people saw her as the old woman she was even though her mind was as sharp as ever.

"I agree that it all sounds suspect when seen through your eyes, Ettie. There are various avenues through which complaints against hospitals are registered. I've checked, and nothing unusual has been reported; certainly nothing of concern."

"Who should make the report, someone from here? If so maybe they were in on it; they wouldn't report themselves, would they? Have any independent investigators actually come here and checked? Will anyone look into Judith's death, for example? You know her son's been talked out of having a post-mortem. They told him it wasn't necessary under the circumstances. To what circumstances were they referring? Surely that's suspect even to you, Detective Crowley."

"When a complaint is registered they will send someone into the hospital, but a complaint hasn't been made. Do you want to lodge a complaint?"

Ettie pushed her lips together firmly. She knew she would sound crazy and not be taken seriously if she said she saw a nurse give an injection in the middle of the night.

She avoided looking at Crowley, but heard his voice in the background saying, "There are many places people can go to who want to make a complaint. There's the Pennsylvania Department of Health who licenses all the hospitals in Pennsylvania. The hospitals need to meet regulations and certain standards of care. There were a few minor complaints about this hospital, but nothing of what you're describing or anything close. Anyone who complains can request their name not be given to the hospital; I checked into that. If anyone had a suspicion such as you do, they're quite within their rights to lodge a complaint. It's when an official complaint is made that they will come into the hospital and inspect the hospital records and ask questions."

Detective Crowley had always been helpful to her and Elsa-May in the past, but apparently not this time. Was it because Judith Morcombe was old and people think that there's nothing too unusual or upsetting when an old person dies? "Won't you even consider for a moment that I'm right? What if Judith was murdered, and she wasn't the first? What if she isn't going to be the last?"

"I have considered it, Ettie. I've given it careful thought, and I've made quite a number of calls. In my opinion, I don't see that there was anything unusual or anything that would lead me to think I have the right to question that woman's death or any other death in this hospital."

She knew she had to find a way to change his mind. If not change his mind she would have him investigate for another reason – any reason. "Crowley, you disappoint me. You've always helped us in the past, and this time should be no different."

"I know you're disappointed, Ettie, but I have to follow protocol. I don't know what else I can do. What would you have me do?"

Ettie threw her hands in the air. "Ask questions of staff in the hospital."

Crowley shook his head. "I've no grounds."

"I spoke to one of the nurses this morning and she thinks that people die suspiciously in this place. She said it always happens on the 8 p.m. to 3 a.m. shift, and she even gave me the name of the person she suspects – a nurse."

"On what grounds does she suspect this nurse? Is she prepared to come forward and make an official complaint and go through the proper channels rather than spread rumors?"

Ettie thought back to her conversation with the young nurse. She had not witnessed anything, and neither was she prepared to come forward. "She said that she wanted to be kept out of it."

"More than likely she's spreading a rumor." A

smile twigged at the corners of Crowley's mouth. "We *Englischers* call things like that an urban myth."

Ettie closed her eyes. She thought she had done well to get so much information from nurse McBride, but was it all for nothing? What would she do if Crowley continued to refuse his help? Who would help if Crowley wouldn't? "The nurse gave me the name of Hadley. The suspect nurse's last name is Hadley; first name is Deirdre. Can you at least check into her background?"

"When Maureen came in and told me about this matter I thought there might be something in what she told me. I spent all morning doing research on the hospital and came up with absolutely nothing. For you, Ettie, I will look into this nurse, but I'm afraid I will be wasting my time."

A smile reached Ettie's lips; she had been successful in coaxing Crowley to look further into things. "Thank you, Detective. Now, I'm afraid I need to have a little sleep. This conversation has tired me out."

He stood awkwardly and tilted his head again. "I'm sorry about your friend. I will look into it as soon as I get back to the office. I know that you and Elsa-May have never been wrong about anything in the past, but I must have grounds to ask those types of questions. You do understand, don't you?"

"Detective Crowley, things like that have not stopped you in the past. You think I'm a silly old lady; I am certain of that."

Crowley stood square on to Ettie and placed his hands on his hips. "Never. I've never thought that you were anything close to silly." Crowley dropped his gaze and said. "Leave it with me. I could always say that I'm asking questions in connection with another matter."

"Yes, good." Ettie leaned forward too fast and her lungs wheezed badly.

"Water?"

Ettie nodded quite unsure why people offered her water every time her lungs wheezed. After she sipped the water and handed the glass back to Crowley, she said, "I will appreciate anything you can do. It must be done quickly. Judith's son's name is Milton Morcombe; I'm not sure where he lives, but he must live somewhere nearby. He came to visit his mother nearly every day while she was in the hospital.

"I'll have a talk to him if that will make you happy. How do you spell Morcombe?" Crowley pulled a small note pad and pen out of his inside, jacket pocket.

Pointing to the other side of the room, Ettie said, "See if it's still written above the bed."

Crowley leaned over. "Ah, yes. It's been rubbed out, but I can just make it out." He jotted the name down on his pad.

"I may be old, Detective Crowley, but I still have all my faculties." Ettie tapped a long, bony finger to her head.

"No doubt, but I've got superiors; I can't be seen to go outside my parameters too far too often." He stuffed the pad and pen back into his pocket. "Enjoy the flowers."

Ettie smiled at him. "Thank you for visiting me

and for helping me once again."

Crowley leaned a little closer. "Ettie, I need you to keep your eyes and ears open. Let me know if you find out anything else. I understand that Bailey is going to stay with you every night?"

"That's right. So, you do think that there might be some truth in what I've said?"

"Like I said, you ladies have been right in the past." Crowley smiled and left Ettie alone in the room.

She was thankful of his visit but wondered why he seemed reluctant to help at first. It must have helped to have Deirdre Hadley's name.

Chapter 7

And he said unto me,
My grace is sufficient for thee:
for my strength is made perfect in weakness.
Most gladly therefore will I rather glory in my
infirmities,
that the power of Christ may rest upon me.
2 Corinthians 12:9

In the afternoon, Elsa-May went home at Ettie's insistence, but Bailey came back to the hospital to visit her.

"What are you doing back here, Bailey? You should be home with Silvie. You can stay tonight again, can't you?"

Bailey nodded. "I've come to see if you need anything. I met Maureen this morning, in Crowley's office."

"*Jah* I know. Crowley's come to see me; he left not long ago." Ettie's chest felt tight, and her head boomed. "*Ach*, Bailey, would you mind opening the window an inch? It's very hot in here, don't you think?"

"*Nee*, not at all. But you do look flushed, Ettie; should I fetch someone?"

"*Nee,*" she snapped, then felt she'd overreacted. "Sorry, I just..." Ettie panicked at the idea of bringing herself to the attention of the possible murderer. But then again, it wasn't between 8 p.m. and 3 a.m., she might be safe.

Bailey turned from the window he'd just opened and frowned. "Whatever is wrong?"

"Nothing. Everything. It's just this place."

Bailey sat down on the edge of Ettie's bed. "I'm not only your nephew, you've become a dear friend to me; I know you're holding back on me. Tell me what's wrong. It isn't your health is it? What did the doctor say? I hope you aren't getting worse."

"*Nee*, I'm mending just fine. It's just that..." Ettie didn't know where to begin and couldn't help herself; the stress of it all finally got to her as she felt she might cry. "*Ach*, Bailey, I didn't want to drag you into another investigation; I know you want to keep out of those types of things."

"What is it, Ettie?"

"Judith, the woman who shared my room."

"You're upset because she died, and you were close to her. I understand."

"*Jah*, but it's not that, Bailey." Ettie blew her nose on the tissue that Bailey handed her from the box on the nightstand. "She received an injection during the night. I can't think what it might have been or why it was given at that time in the morning. I mean, she was due to go home; she had recovered completely and was sleeping soundly. And then in the morning, she was dead."

Bailey stroked a stray lock of hair away from Ettie's face. "I know all of that, Ettie. That's why I stayed with you last night."

Ettie looked at her nephew pleadingly and blinked rapidly. "Bailey, am I the only person who thinks that Judith was murdered? The hospital must be covering it up."

Bailey stared at her without saying a word.

"You think I'm crazy don't you? Some doddering

silly old woman scared of her own shadow."

"Ettie, if you think that's what happened, so do I."

The relief in her heart released the tension around her chest, and Ettie gasped, letting go of a sigh. "You do? *Ach,* you don't know how good it is to hear that. Why did I ever doubt you?"

"You can't get upset like this. Why don't you come back home with me? Silvie and I can take care of you."

Ettie shook her head. "I must stay. *Gott* might have put me here for a reason. I didn't know whether to tell you about this or not since you left the FBI. You thought you'd left all those things behind you; I'm sure."

"Don't be concerned about me. If you don't want to come home to my *haus,* we could have a nurse come visit you at your home."

"*Nee*, I've stumbled across this and *Gott* must want me to do something about it."

"Who else have you told?" Bailey asked.

"Crowley looked at me like I imagined

everything. Is it because I'm old, I wonder? When you get old, people treat you differently; almost as if you're a child. I notice some of the nurses speak to me as if I'm five-years-old. Others speak loudly as if I'm deaf when my hearing is perfect. I'm sure others assume that I've simply lost my mind. When you're young, you never quite believe you're going to get old and wrinkly." Ettie stared at the ceiling. "Sometimes I feel I've been put out to pasture like an old cow."

Ettie lifted up her hand and studied it. "I remember looking at my *grossmammi's* old hand and thinking how awful it looked." She twisted and turned her hand. "Now, look at mine, wrinkled and spotted. The same as the one I thought looked horrible, and now it's mine." Ettie put her arm down beside her.

"I guess people don't grasp that they'll be old someday too."

Ettie managed a little laugh. "Bailey you're not yet fifty, and you're talking as if you're as old as me."

Bailey smiled and then said, "I'm much older

than I feel, I'm sure. Anyway, I'd prefer to keep out of the things you mentioned. Crowley can handle it; he knows what he's doing."

"*Jah*, Bailey, I never meant you to get involved at all; I just felt the need to tell you. In the end, Crowley agreed to help, but he seemed most reluctant."

After Bailey asked more questions, Ettie felt free to tell him all that young nurse Melanie McBride told her.

"Silvie was going to stay the night with you after she finishes work, but I'd feel better if I stayed the night. She's upset that she hasn't been to see you."

"I feel safer with you here, Bailey. Tell Silvie that I appreciate her letting you stay here with me. I'll see her soon."

"I'll sleep here the next night too."

"Would you?"

Bailey stood up and patted Ettie's hand. "*Jah*, of course, I will. I'll come back after dinner."

Ettie sighed in relief.

* * *

After Bailey left the next morning, Ettie was pleased to see the light of day. No one had given her an injection in the middle of the night. She looked over at the still empty bed and missed her friend.

"Morning, Ettie."

It was young nurse McBride.

"Nurse," Ettie whispered.

The nurse frowned and came closer. "Yes?"

"I have a detective friend looking into the things you told me about."

The nurse drew back, opened her mouth and looked over her shoulder at the doorway.

Ettie continued, "I thought I should let you know because you've been so nice to me. If they find out who did it, people, who have kept quiet, will go down as accomplices."

The nurse frowned and put her head to one side. "Go down?"

Ettie nodded. "Withholding information is considered a very serious crime in this country."

"Well, I don't know anything."

"You mentioned people died who you thought shouldn't have."

The nurse looked behind her, to the door again. "That was nothing really."

"Nothing? It didn't sound like it was nothing when you told me all those things just yesterday." Ettie noticed the nurse's hands trembling. "I wouldn't want you to get into any trouble with the law."

The nurse licked her lips, stared at Ettie for a moment and said, "I get off at 3 p.m. I'll come back and talk to you then."

Even though Ettie had visitors through the day, she could not get her mind off the nurse who was coming back at three that afternoon.

* * *

At ten minutes past three, the nurse, Melanie McBride, came back into Ettie's room.

"I don't want to get into any trouble. I told you all the deaths happen on the eight to three shift. The people who died were all over fifty."

Ettie raised an eyebrow. "How many do you know of?"

"I guess twenty."

"Twenty?" Ettie drew the sheet up closer to her neck. "And what are the names of these people who died in this way?"

"My friend Janet told our superior about nurse Hadley; then she was transferred to another hospital. They told her if they opened an investigation that would leave the hospital open to millions of dollars of law suites."

"The hospital knows of Nurse Hadley and what's been happening?"

The nurse nodded. "They do; her name's been mentioned to them, but they might not believe it. I can't say anything more; I need my job. Besides, I don't even know whether my suspicions are valid. It might be sheer coincidence."

"Can you get me names of the people who died?" Melanie looked away.

"Time is getting away from us, Melanie."

"I thought you'd ask me for them. I'll give them

to you. But, I need my name kept out of it. I don't want to get into any trouble - with anyone."

Ettie nodded.

Nurse McBride pulled a list of names from her pocket. "Here, I could only find these. I can look another day, but they'll wonder why I'm on the computer if I stayed on any longer today."

Ettie ran her eyes over the list. Judith's name and her son's number were on the top of the list. Reading down the list, next to every name was the name and phone number of the next of kin. "Thank you, Melanie. Well done."

Melanie left Ettie's room just as Maureen came through the door. "Morning, Ettie. I've got cakes."

The last thing Ettie needed right now was cake. "Maureen, get this list to Crowley at once Tell him that a nurse has given me names of people she considers died suspicious deaths."

"*Ach, jah*, of course." Maureen popped the cakes down and took the list from Ettie. "The station isn't far away. I'll take the list to him and come back to see you. Did you find out the nurse's name; the one you suspect?"

"Deidre Hadley. I've already given her name to Crowley."

Maureen nodded and hurried out the door.

Chapter 8

Therefore, I urge you, brothers,
in view of God's mercy,
to offer your bodies as living sacrifices,
holy and pleasing to God—
this is your spiritual act of worship.
Romans 12:1

Sitting in his office, Crowley pondered over the situation involving Ettie and the unexplained deaths. He had felt guilty not being able to offer more in the way of assistance. Now that a nurse had come forward and named names, he felt comfortable doing more digging around. He examined the list of names that Maureen had just given him.

After considering the names, telephone numbers and addresses, Crowley found himself staring at his phone for several moments before he picked up the receiver. He decided to call Judith's family first.

The phone rang enough times to have Crowley prepared to hang up before it was finally answered.

"Hello." A male with a strained voice answered.

"Hello, my name is Detective Crowley. I'm looking for Milton Morcombe, son of Judith Morcombe."

There was a distinct pause before the male on the other end of the line replied, "Speaking."

"Sorry to disturb you, but I've been following up on some administration work for the hospital where Mrs. Morcombe was admitted. We have some details missing regarding how she was referred."

"You said you are a detective? What's this about?"

"Your answers might assist us on a confidential matter we're investigating."

"There's not a problem, is there?"

"No, not at all," Crowley said. "Just routine questions."

"All right then. Well, we originally took my mother to the emergency department. She wasn't feeling too well; we were concerned about her blood pressure. It had been causing her some problems these past few months. After we arrived and spoke to a doctor, he referred her onto the hospital ward. We were assured it was nothing dangerous." He cleared his throat. "Is that the type of information you were looking for?"

"I appreciate how difficult this time must be for you, Mr. Morcombe. Thank you for your help."

"No problem, no problem at all, Detective. I hope I gave you information that was helpful."

"Yes, but one more thing, Mr. Morcombe, I can see by the hospital records that we've had to subpoena, over another matter that you did not ask for an autopsy; can I ask why?"

"I was going to, but the nurse I talked to at the hospital said it wasn't warranted due to her age."

"And how old was your mother?"

"Just turned sixty."

Crowley raised his eyebrows, he was not far off sixty himself. "And she was in good health other than her blood pressure?"

"What's this about? What's your name again,

Detective?"

Detective Crowley rubbed his forehead, hoping that helping the widows would not get him into trouble. "Detective Crowley."

"And what exactly are you investigating?"

"I'm not at liberty to discuss it, I'm sorry. Well, thank you for your time, Mr. Morcombe."

"Not at all."

After the call was done, Crowley heaved a sigh of relief. Until he remembered he still had six other phone numbers to call.

* * *

When Maureen arrived back at the hospital, she knew she had to do something to help. Ettie had told her the name of the nurse she suspected, so how could she find out more about her?

She approached a nurse who was sitting behind a desk in Ettie's ward. Maureen knew this nurse was not nurse Hadley or nurse McBride. "Is Nurse Hadley here?" Maureen knew that nurse Hadley would not be there as it was too early for her shift.

The nurse looked up from her computer. "Ah, I don't think so. I'll just have a look to see when she's on next." She pressed a few buttons on the console. "She's on the late shift; she'll be here at 8 p.m."

"Oh dear, I wanted to thank her for being so good to my friend Judith."

"Yes, I'm sorry to hear about that." The nurse smiled and looked suitably sympathetic.

"Nurse Hadley was good to her; she's such a caring nurse." Maureen leaned on the counter top. "You know, there's not many people around these days who truly care."

The nurse nodded.

"Do you know much about nurse Hadley?"

"I know her from working with her."

"What's she really like?" Maureen placed her elbows on the counter.

"She's…"

"Does she have children?" Maureen interrupted, helping the young nurse as she struggled to find words.

"No, she just got married."

"Wonderful, she married a doctor, did she?" Maureen giggled hoping the nurse would think she was enjoying a gossip.

The nurse laughed with her. "No, she didn't. She married a man who owns a funeral parlor."

Maureen drew back a little in shock. "A funeral parlor?"

The nurse covered her mouth to stifle another laugh. She looked around about her and then said in a low voice, "We joke that she has a place to send her mistakes."

"I'm sure she wouldn't have many mistakes though. Not a good nurse like her."

"There are some who say that her husband only married her so he could get more dead bodies. You know, improve his business." The nurse laughed louder.

"Oh, I see," Maureen said before an older nurse approached the two of them.

The older nurse appeared stern. Had the old

nurse heard her conversation with the young nurse? Maureen knew that was the end of the information she would get with the stony-faced nurse around. "Well, I might be around to see nurse Hadley and thank her myself."

The young nurse nodded.

Maureen walked away and hid around the corner from the nurses' station.

She heard the older nurse say, "Were you talking about Hadley just now?"

The younger nurse replied, "That Amish lady was saying what a good nurse she was."

"That's a joke. There have been more deaths since she's been on this ward."

The young nurse said, "Maybe she is drumming up business for her new husband."

"Humph, either that or they're doing illegal trade in body organs."

"Yeah, would be perfect with her brother being a doctor in the emergency department." The young nurse giggled. "There would be plenty of spare parts."

Maureen moved away so she would not be seen.

* * *

"Detective Crowley, what have you found out?"

The detective walked further into the room and sat down in the chair beside Ettie's bed."

"You don't look very happy." After Ettie had spoken, she realized that the detective always had the same expression on his face, but something told her that he was about to tell her something important.

"I phoned several next of kin of those people on the list. It appears there are common threads with the deaths."

"The people whose names I gave you from the young nurse?"

"Yes. They were all admitted to the emergency department in the first instance."

Ettie heaved a sigh of relief. She had been admitted from her doctor directly into the ward. "I feel a little safer."

"Is it possible for me to speak to the nurse you were speaking with?"

Ettie shook her head. "Understandably she's nervous, and she values her job. One of her friends said something, but they transferred her."

"We need someone to issue a formal complaint," Crowley said.

Maureen entered the room and stood at the end of Ettie's bed. "I've just found something out, but you two continue with your conversation; I'll wait."

Ettie said to detective Crowley, "Are you sure that no one has ever filed a complaint about one of these deaths? The nurse said there were around twenty that she knows of."

"Not one has been filed."

"What about the nurse whose name I gave you - Deirdre Hadley?"

"I'll be checking into her background when I get back to the station. The thing I don't understand is why would someone kill people? Would it be a crazed serial killer working in the hospital? It does seem far-fetched, but stranger things have happened."

Maureen saw her chance. "I found out something interesting about her."

"About Deirdre Hadley?" Ettie asked.

Maureen nodded.

"What is it?" Crowley asked.

Maureen moved around the same side of the bed as detective Crowley. Lowering her voice, she said, "She recently married a man who owns a funeral parlor, and her brother works as a doctor in this hospital's emergency department."

Ettie smiled and turned to Crowley. "Sounds as if that gives you a little more to go on, Detective."

Crowley nodded. "Yes, it does. A few more common threads, and more people to follow up on. Good work in finding that out, Maureen."

Maureen smiled revealing the slight gap between her two front teeth.

"Ah, now you're interested, aren't you? I'm not just a silly old lady." Ettie turned to Maureen. "Detective Crowley just told me that all the people who nurse McBride thought died suspiciously all came to the hospital through the emergency department before they were admitted to the ward."

"I never said, and I have never thought you were a silly old lady, Ettie. I did say I'd never known your instincts to be wrong." The detective's thin lips turned upwards at the corners. "Having said all that, do you think you'd be better off away from this place under the circumstances?"

"No," Ettie said firmly. "If I left now and more people fell victim to whatever is happening in this hospital, I could never live with myself knowing there might have been something I could have done to help."

"Are you sure?" Crowley asked. "There's danger involved. Even if you're safe from whoever is targeting these patients, you could still find yourself in a difficult situation."

"I always feel safe no matter where I am. I'd rather not be here, but I feel that I must stay. We need to get to the bottom of this and it's much easier if I'm here," Ettie said.

Detective Crowley frowned and glanced at Maureen. "These things are best left to professionals. I've got enough to go on from here; thanks to you two."

"Let us know if you want our help with anything else," Maureen said.

"One more thing, Maureen. You didn't make your questions too obvious, did you? We don't want to arouse suspicion."

"I happened to overhear a conversation. They laughed about her being married to a funeral director." Maureen stood straight and held her chin high.

"Excellent; that was a stroke of luck," Crowley said.

Ettie looked at him through narrowed eyes. "Luck, detective?"

"Yes, I forgot; you ladies always find help from on high." Crowley stood up.

Ettie and Maureen shot each other a smile.

"If you two ladies will excuse me, I'll go and do some research."

"I appreciate everything you're doing, Crowley, thank you," Ettie said.

"Before you go, Detective," Maureen said as the detective was nearly out the door.

"Yes?" He swiveled on his heel.

"The reason the ladies were giggling about the funeral parlor and the nurse marrying the funeral director was something to do with selling body organs. Does that mean anything to you?"

The detective took a giant step toward Maureen. "What did they say?"

"Just that; that's all I heard. The nurse married the funeral director, and they said that he's probably involved with selling body organs; and something about having spare parts to sell. At first, they were saying she was sending her mistakes there, and he was getting extra business; then they talked about the body parts."

"I see."

"What is it?" Ettie said pushing herself up onto her elbows. "What does it all mean?"

The detective sighed. "I had begun to think it

might be illegal black-market trade in body parts, but I didn't want to mention it to you ladies. I read something of it recently in one of the police journals. There was an arrest of a funeral director illegally obtaining body organs and selling them to people who were on waiting lists for organ transplants." He looked at the two widows then continued, "There's a shortage of organs and when people die and they have nominated their organs can be used after their death, someone on the transplant list can get a cornea or a kidney, maybe a heart."

Ettie nodded. "And you think that's what could be happening here? When they have too long to wait they look at illegal means of getting what they need?"

"I hope not, but due to the amount of money involved it is becoming more wide spread. I'm certain I read that a kidney can be sold for as much as $180,000. When someone's facing death, all perspective of money goes out the window. There would be some people who'd be prepared to do anything to extend their life." The detective scratched his chin. "Then there are people who are willing to facilitate obtaining the organs and these unscrupulous people profit highly from doing so."

"What are you thinking, Detective? If we're on the trail of something like that then the nurse, her brother and her new husband could be in something together," Maureen said.

Ettie put her hand against her head. "*Ach*, that's horrid. I never knew of the existence of such technology."

"It's amazing what they can do, Ettie and unfortunately there's always going to be people who will take advantage of another's pain." Without another word, Crowley left the room.

Ettie was silent.

"What is it, Ettie?" Maureen asked.

"Which nurses were you speaking to?"

"I was speaking to a young one I haven't seen before and an older one with a cranky face."

"The older one with the cranky face would be nurse Bush. Was the younger nurse Melanie McBride?"

Maureen's gaze shot to the ceiling. "Nurse McBride is the young one who comes in every morning, isn't she?"

"*Jah*, the pretty young nurse; she's always happy."

"*Nee* she wasn't the one I was talking to."

Ettie tapped her finger on her chin. "Nurse McBride gave me Hadley's name and told me about the people who died. Why didn't Melanie ever mention that Hadley had just married a funeral director or that her brother was a doctor here?"

"Maybe she didn't want to get too involved?"

Ettie pressed her lips together, and her eyebrows drew closer. "I suspect there might be another reason that nurse McBride gave me just a drop of information."

Hurrying to sit on the chair next to Ettie's bed, Maureen asked, "What are you thinking? She seems such a lovely girl. You don't think she's involved with all this business, do you?"

Ettie's brow furrowed. "I don't know – yet."

Chapter 9

To every thing there is a season,
and a time to every purpose under the heaven:
A time to be born, and a time to die; a time to plant,
and a time to pluck up that which is planted;
Ecclesiastes 3:1

Crowley rubbed his chin. How could he obtain a warrant from a judge to search the funeral parlor? He would sound unprofessional to speak of black-market body parts, hospital rumors, the newly married nurse and the midnight injection. Put all those elements together and to Crowley that was enough to get a warrant, but to a judge that was a different matter. Judges did not endorse warrants on hunches or suspicions of the police. He had to have more.

Once Crowley reached his car in the hospital car park, he knew what he had to do. He had to have Milton Morcombe agree to an autopsy. If Milton signed a document allowing one, the paramedics could take Judith's body from the funeral parlor to a medical examiner. *Yes, that will work, but it will need to be done quickly.*

Crowley sped back to his office to get Milton's home address. Once he had it, he sat in his office wondering how he could convince Milton to allow an autopsy of his mother's body when days ago he had decided against one. What would it take for Milton to change his mind? Maureen's wide smile came into Crowley's mind.

If anyone could talk someone into doing something, it would be Maureen with her charming smile and easy manner. Standard protocol would demand he take a policewoman from his station if he wanted a more gentle approach. Crowley opted with his gut instinct; he would have Maureen accompany him to speak with Milton Morcombe.

Before Crowley did another thing, he searched for the article on black-market body parts that he had recently seen. He opened the large bottom drawer where he kept his police journals. They were organized by date; they were not filed alphabetically. Crowley considered having someone come in and rearrange his filing system as he sifted through the selection of papers.

When he found the article, he leaned back in his chair. Scanning down to the middle of the article, he read:

In February 2013, Compton, the owner of a Philadelphia crematorium pleaded guilty to illegal tissue and an organ harvesting.

Prosecutors said that the defendant provided the president of Biochemical Research Laboratories with 188 corpses for just under $200,000.

Compton pleaded guilty to criminal conspiracy by the illegal taking and selling of corpses connected to a tissue and organ-harvesting scheme.

There was more to the article, but that was enough for Crowley. He filed it back into his drawer and turned his attention to his computer. He did a general Internet search on illegal organ harvesting and found:

In the past victims of criminal forced organ harvesting were routinely executed with a shot to the head before their organs were harvested. Later, an injection method was developed wherein the victim would be given an injection that would paralyze their body, thus yielding organs in better condition for transplantation.

International human rights lawyer, James Pinto, investigated forced organ harvesting in China was quoted by a major newspaper saying that, "They are not killing by injection, they are harvesting the organs of the body while that body is paralyzed, but still legally alive."

When he read about the paralyzing injection, Crowley was more sure that Ettie was onto something. The nurse could well have given Judith Morcombe an injection to paralyze her. He moved on to another Internet search to read:

In the United States, the sale of body organs is illegal as in most countries of the world. A chronic shortage of legal transplant organs has led to a thriving black-market organ trade Internationally. Often donors from Third World countries are offered thousands of dollars in exchange for organs that are then sold on for a larger profit to wealthy recipients, more often than not the recipients are from the First World. There have been reports that donors from Third World countries who have sold a kidney for the promise of large sums have not been paid.

There was a photo accompanying the article of four men from a Third World country showing scars from their operations. The same four men claim they were each promised $1,500. - $2,000. but they were never paid.

Crowley ripped off the sheet of paper with Milton's address and shoving it in his pocket he headed out of the police station. He hoped that Maureen would agree to go with him.

Once Crowley was back in Ettie's hospital room, he was relived to see that Maureen was still there.

After he asked Maureen to go with him to talk to Milton, she said, "I don't know the man, Detective. I've never met him. I think I noticed him visiting his mother, but I never spoke to him."

Ettie interrupted, "See what you can do, Maureen.

He's a very nice man and tell him I said hello."

Maureen shrugged her shoulders. "I'll see what I can do. I'll help if I can."

"Good. We've not much time to waste," Crowley said as he marched toward the door.

* * *

Just as Maureen and the detective left Ettie alone, bishop Paul and his wife Mary came to visit. It was comforting for Ettie to see the bishop with his dark, bushy beard and the small Mary with her sweet smile.

"It's lovely that you've both come to see me," Ettie said pleased to have visitors now she was feeling better.

Mary sat in the chair next to Ettie's bed, and bishop Paul took a chair from the other side of the room and placed it next to his wife.

The bishop's wife took Ettie's hand. "You're in our prayers."

"*Denke*."

"Elsa-May told us you were in here," bishop Paul said as he looked around the room.

"Hospitals are my least favorite place; it's *gut* to see some familiar faces," Ettie said.

"You've not had many visitors then?" the bishop asked.

"*Jah*, I have. I just miss being at home, and I miss my dog Ginger. I miss being outside; I haven't been outside for days."

"How long do you think you'll be in here?" Mary asked.

Ettie thought of Judith dying and how she wanted to get out of the hospital as fast as she possibly could. She could not tell either of them about what happened; they would not want to be entangled with the problems of the world. Ettie smiled at Mary. "Not much longer, I'm certain of that."

"We will miss you at the gatherings," the bishop said.

Their conversation was strained. Ettie knew that they were doing their duty in visiting her; after all, they weren't her close friends, they were Elsa-

May's friends. The bishop's wife was most likely Elsa-May's closest friend in the community. Ettie felt that she never had much in common with the bishop's *fraa*.

After an awkward silence, the bishop said, "Is there anything we can get you?"

"*Nee*. Elsa-May comes in every day, so do Maureen and Bailey. Emma comes in too, but not as often." Ettie realized she forgot her manners. "Would you like some tea? There's a visitors' room not far away. You can make some tea and bring it back here."

Bishop Paul said he'd fetch the tea, and he left Mary to talk to Ettie.

"You do look a little pale, Ettie."

"I've been quite sick. They say pneumonia is quite serious. Doctor says I'm out of the danger zone now."

"Do your *kinner* know? Wilhelm is going to Ohio tomorrow, and he can let them know." Wilhelm was one of Paul and Mary's sons.

"*Nee*, it would only worry them; no need to cause

them concern. They'd make a trip here for nothing. I'd be out of hospital and home before they even arrived. I'd rather they not know. Although, I know, they'll hear about it soon." It never took long for news to spread between communities.

The bishop came through the door clutching three mugs of steaming, hot tea. He set them down on the metal set of drawers next to Ettie. "Do you have milk, Ettie? I'll go back and fetch some if you do."

"*Nee*, I'll have it as it comes." After they all had a mouthful of tea, Ettie said, "Tea-bags just don't taste the same, do they?"

The bishop and his wife murmured their agreements.

Half an hour of forced conversation later, the bishop and his *fraa* said goodbye to Ettie and left. Ettie was grateful for their visit and their prayers; she would need their prayers now she was staying longer in the hospital.

Chapter 10

And whatsoever ye do, do it heartily,
as to the Lord, and not unto men;
Colossians 3:23

Twenty minutes after they left the hospital, Maureen and detective Crowley were at the home of Milton Morcombe. After Crowley told him who they were, Milton asked them inside.

"I'm sorry to arrive without calling you first." Crowley apologized for not being truthful with him when he phoned earlier. He told Milton the whole story surrounding the midnight injection, the nurse, the recent marriage of the suspected nurse to the funeral director and the hospital rumors. Then Crowley approached the subject of an autopsy.

"I don't know. She's due to be cremated tomorrow," Milton said.

Maureen leaned forward toward him. "Milton, if what the detective suspects is correct, do you think your mother would want you to find out what happened?"

Milton nervously drummed his fingers on his dining room table. "She missed her cats. All she wanted was to come home and be with them."

Crowley and Maureen glanced at each other.

"One thing my mother hated was injustice. She couldn't see a person disadvantaged even on a television show." He tipped his head upward and blinked back tears. "What do you want me to do?"

Crowley said, "Once you sign these documents that will give me the authority to have an autopsy performed. Naturally we hope that nothing untoward has happened, but if it has we need to track down those responsible."

Milton put his hand out for the papers. "I suppose that's what mother would want."

Once Milton signed the document, Crowley and Maureen left Milton's house and made their way to the funeral parlor. "When we get there, don't get out of the car. By the time we arrive, there'll be ambulance and police cars waiting."

Just as he said, there was one ambulance and

three police cars waiting when they arrived at the funeral home. He hoped that Mr. Hadley would not have had time to destroy evidence, although without a search warrant all Crowley could do was take Judith's body away.

"Don't be concerned with me, Detective. I'm happy to wait here."

"I'll see you in a few minutes, Maureen." Crowley left his car and marched to the door, followed by four police officers.

A balding man in his sixties opened the door. "We're closed; I'm sorry." He went to shut the door, but Crowley wedged his foot in it. The man looked down at Crowley's foot and then looked up at his face. "What's all this about?"

"Are you Mr. Hadley?"

"Yes."

Crowley showed the piece of paper. "I've got an order to take the body of Judith Morcombe."

"No. We've got the rights to her cremation. You can't take her."

Crowley waved the paper in the air. "I'm afraid

this overrules whatever instruction you've had. I can always get a warrant and search this place top to bottom and take Mrs. Morcombe's body. Is that what you'd prefer?"

Hadley stared at Crowley and then stepped aside. The four police officers followed Crowley inside; two paramedics with a stretch were close behind. Hadley had no choice but to show them directly to Judith's body.

When Judith's body was safely out of the building, Crowley turned to Mr. Hadley. "There will be police officers watching this place. Don't think about doing anything stupid."

"I don't know what you're talking about. You still haven't told me what any of this is about."

Crowley ignored him, turned and walked back to his car. "Well, that's done," he said to Maureen. "Now, I just wait for a phone call to tell us what the autopsy reveals."

Maureen's eyes grew wide. "What happened?"

"Hadley was not happy to see us. He said he did not know the whereabouts of his wife." Crowley breathed out heavily. "Anyway, we can't make any arrests until we find out what the autopsy reveals. The way he acted, I know that he's guilty of something. Now, Maureen, can I drive you home or would you like me to take you back to the hospital?"

Maureen looked up at the nearly dark sky. "Could you take me home, Detective?"

"You caught a taxi to the hospital?"

"Yes, it's too far for the buggy." Maureen glanced over at Crowley. "You look worried, Detective."

"I've taken a punt and I'm hoping it pays off. I couldn't have gotten a warrant with no solid information, but if what you overheard is correct, Judith's body will be evidence enough."

"Milton said that his mother was due to be cremated tomorrow."

Crowley raised his eyebrows. "Yes; that will have to be delayed now."

"Exactly, and they've had the body for days, if they were going to do anything they would have done so by now." Maureen looked out the window.

When Crowley stopped the car outside Maureen's house, Maureen turned to him. "I have apple cake, would you like some?"

Detective Crowley smiled and looked at his watch.

"I mean, to take with you. It's too close to dinner time to have cake."

"Thank you, Maureen. I'd love some."

"Come inside and I'll package it up for you."

The detective walked into Maureen's home and followed her into the kitchen.

"You've never been here before, have you, Detective?"

Detective Crowley smiled. "Ronald, please call me Ronald. No, I've never been here."

"Have a seat, Ronald."

Detective Crowley sat at the kitchen table, amused that Maureen appeared to be uncomfortable with calling him Ronald. Everyone was always so official with him either calling him Detective, Crowley or Detective Crowley. He'd given almost his whole life to the job and had few friends.

Hearing someone refer to him as Ronald would be a welcome change. "How long have you been by yourself, Maureen?"

"My husband died a good many years ago. He was a very sick man. We had two good years together before his health failed. I took care of him for ten years before the Lord took him home."

"Sorry to hear that, Maureen. It must have been hard for you. He was a lucky man to have you to care for him."

Maureen looked up from cutting a large section of cake and gave him a large smile.

He wondered what it would be like to have a woman like Maureen to come home to. Should he suggest that he join her for a meal at some stage since they were both on their own? He'd always liked Maureen and found her easy to talk to. What if she said no? That would make things awkward since he was friendly with the five widows. Maybe she could not say yes due to the Amish beliefs of keeping separate from *Englischers*. Either way, it was most likely not a good idea to ask.

"There you are, Detective. I mean, Ronald."

Detective Crowley stood up and took the container from Maureen. "Thank you; it's very kind of you."

"I know how much you enjoy your cakes."

"I'll let you know how the autopsy went. I'll get a call tonight and I'll go by the hospital tomorrow morning and let Ettie know."

Maureen followed the detective to the door.

Crowley walked quickly to his car and before he opened his door he gave Maureen a wave.

She waved to him and as he drove away, he watched Maureen in his rear view mirror.

* * *

Maureen had always liked Detective Crowley's calm, slow manner. In that way, he reminded her of her late husband. He was easy to be around and she missed having someone to care for. She thought for a moment that he was thinking the same, but he never let on as much.

She shook her head. *What are you thinking you silly woman? A man like Crowley would never become Amish and I would never leave my community and my friends*, she thought. Maureen giggled out aloud. How would she ever get used to calling Crowley, Ronald? She never even wondered what his first name might be. She would call him Crowley or Detective in front of the other widows.

It was unusual for Maureen not to cook herself a proper dinner, but tonight she wasn't hungry. She sliced herself the chicken that she had saved earlier and made herself a chicken and relish sandwich. She needed something in her stomach. After her sandwich, she sat in her living room with a cup of nettle tea.

She looked around about her and wondered what Crowley would have thought of her humble, small *haus*. She had to sell her large house after her husband died. They had expected to have a large *familye* when they were married, but *Gott* had other plans.

Maureen regretted never having *kinner*, but that

must have been *Gott's* will. Maybe her recently married friends, Emma or Silvie would have *kinner* soon and she would be close to them and be like their aunt.

* * *

Just as Ettie closed her eyes a male nurse came into the room. He looked down at the clipboard in his hands. "Mrs. Ettie Smith?"

"Yes."

"I've come to fetch you for your x-ray."

Ettie could not remember her doctor mentioning another x-ray to her. She had one the first day she arrived at the hospital. "There must be a mistake. My doctor said nothing about an x-ray."

The nurse looked down at his board again. "We've got you down for one this afternoon." He leaned forward and raised his eyebrows. "Perhaps you forgot?"

Ettie frowned at the nurse.

She was about to say that being old did not

necessarily mean she was also forgetful when he said, "I'll go and get a wheelchair; it's at the other end of the hospital. Or would you rather me wheel you in the bed?"

"Oh, no. A wheelchair would be better."

The nurse was gone for a few minutes and returned with a wheelchair. He helped Ettie into it and a few minutes later, she was in a different wing of the hospital. "They'll call me when you're finished to take you back to your ward. Wait here, they'll call your name shortly."

Ettie looked around the empty waiting room. There were the usual side-tables with out-of-date magazines and the same paintings on the walls that Ettie had seen in other areas of the hospital. As she waited, she wondered why her doctor had never mentioned another x-ray. Something seemed odd.

"Mrs. Smith?" A young woman who Ettie had never seen before stepped into the waiting room. She wore a different uniform to the nurses and Ettie thought that she must be a radiographer rather than a nurse.

"Smith, that's me."

The young woman wheeled Ettie into the x-ray room. "Nurse won't be a moment."

Ettie remained silent as the woman left the room. The door opened a minute later and Ettie looked up in horror to see Deirdre Hadley walk through the door. She had never known for sure that this nurse was Deirdre Hadley, but her instincts told her that it was. Ettie gulped and tried not to look nervous. If she was right, this woman was a killer, and she was alone with her. Worse still, none of her relatives, friends or detective Crowley knew where she was. No one could help her. It was a rare moment that Ettie wished she had the strength of her youth. This woman would have no trouble in overpowering her now frail, elderly body. *Gott, help me*, Ettie prayed silently.

Deirdre sat beside her. "So Mrs. Smith, how are you?"

Ettie coughed. "I've got pneumonia apparently. I didn't know my doctor ordered an x-ray."

"Why did you have a detective visit you; is he

a friend of yours?" Deirdre's green eyes opened wider then narrowed as her head twisted to the side.

A chill ran through Ettie, but she knew she had to stay calm. "Yes, quite a good friend."

"Your other friend, the fat one, she's been asking questions about me, I hear."

Ettie knew the nurse was speaking of Maureen. "I wouldn't call her fat. I'd say she was pleasantly plump. She's a good cook; I'll have her bring in some cake for you."

"I don't care about cake," the woman hissed like a snake. "Why was she asking questions about me?"

"I have no idea. Perhaps you should ask her yourself."

"You're holding back something from me, Mrs. Smith."

Anger rose within Ettie. This woman had killed someone and now Ettie knew that it was not an assumption; by the actions of the woman, it was a fact. Ettie figured she had nothing to lose; she was old and would soon die anyway. "Why did I see you giving Judith an injection the night she died?"

The nurse stood up and yelled. "I did no such thing. Who have you been speaking to? You better not have told anyone that. Did you tell that detective friend of yours?"

"It's all over the hospital; everyone knows what you do." Ettie figured that her best chance would be to make the nurse think that everyone knew what she was up to. "It's just a matter of time before the police get you."

The woman drew her hand back and smacked Ettie across her face. "What do you mean by that?"

Ettie's heard her neck crack and felt her face sting. She tried not to show how much it hurt. She moved her neck and was relieved that her neck had not broken. "You'll go to jail for a long time."

The nurse stretched out her hands towards Ettie but snapped them back in fright when her cell phone rang. "What is it?" she barked at the caller.

Ettie listened hard and heard the caller on the other end yelling, "Get out of there now. The police have just been here; they've taken one of the bodies."

Hadley clicked her flip-top cell phone shut, gave Ettie an evil glare before she ran out the door.

Ettie knew Crowley was close to finding the truth. It seemed he had been successful in having Milton agree to the autopsy. She wheeled herself over to a large, red button on the side of the room and pressed it. The words under the button said 'call.' She picked up her chart that one of the staff had left on the table. Ettie saw that it was Nurse Hadley who had ordered her x-ray.

After waiting a while, Ettie realized that no one was coming for her. Ettie pushed on the wheels at the side of her chair and managed to wheel herself out the door. She wheeled herself through the waiting room and into the hospital corridor. Which way had the nurse brought her? Should she turn left or right? All the stark corridors looked the same.

"Can I help you?" an approaching nurse asked Ettie.

"I've lost my way; I'm supposed to be in Ward D."

The nurse smiled. "I'll take you there."

The nurse took Ettie back to her ward and helped her get back into bed. "What were you doing so far away?"

"I thought I'd take a look around." Ettie smiled back at her trying to appear as though she were a vague old lady.

As she pulled the sheet up over Ettie, the nurse asked, "Is there a reason that one side of your face is very red?"

With her fingertips, Ettie touched her still stinging face. "It could be a rash or could be one of my allergies."

The nurse seemed to be satisfied with Ettie's answer. Ettie knew she could not tell the nurse anything about Deirdre. She could not tell anyone anything until Crowley was able to get that warrant. Ettie hoped she hadn't ruined Crowley's chance of catching Deirdre and all those involved with her. For her own safety's sake she had to have Deirdre think that everyone knew about her.

After the helpful nurse left, Ettie relaxed in her

bed. "*Denke, Gott,*" she said aloud, "for saving me from that wicked woman." She thought back over what the wicked nurse had said. She said that Maureen had been asking questions about her, but she was sure that Maureen had said that she overheard conversations about the nurse. Ettie knew for certain now that Deirdre Hadley was guilty. She closed her eyes to rest, but there were too many questions swirling in her mind.

Why had Deirdre sent her for an x-ray? Was she going to give her a lethal injection once she was alone in the room with her, or just ask questions? What if Deirdre came back now and found her alone in the room? Ettie reached for the phone and called her nephew Bailey. She would have him come and stay with her.

Chapter 11

Be sober, be vigilant; because your
adversary the devil,
as a roaring lion, walketh about,
seeking whom he may devour:
1 Peter 5:8

Ettie woke the next morning to see Bailey fast asleep in the chair next to her. He'd been good to her since she'd been ill. She had forbidden Elsa-May to tell her five *kinner* that she was sick enough to be in the hospital. None of her children were in the same community. Three of Ettie's sons were in Ohio. It wouldn't be long before gossip reached them, but Ettie figured she would most likely be out of hospital when it did. Ettie's two *dochders* had left the community when they were teenagers; Ettie had no idea where they were and it had been ten years since they had contacted her.

Ettie looked up to the ceiling and wondered if her *kinner* would be upset when she died. Did they even love her as she had loved her *mudder* and *vadder*? She did not feel as though they did even though she loved them and had done the best as a *mudder* to them. What had forced her *dochders* out of the community into the *Englisch* world? Her sons had married women in an Amish community in Ohio. All her sons had *kinner,* but what of her *dochders*? She had no idea about them. What if she died and never learned what became of them? Maybe Crowley could find out.

She had heard nothing the previous evening from either Crowley or Maureen and just as she was getting worried, Crowley walked through the door.

"Crowley, it can't be seven yet," Ettie said a little too loudly and woke Bailey.

Bailey Rivers blinked and stretched his hands above his head. "I can't believe I slept. Morning, Crowley."

Crowley nodded his head. "Rivers."

"I'll leave you two alone. Silvie's working this morning and I want to see her before she goes."

Bailey stood up then leaned over and kissed Ettie on her cheek before he walked out the door.

Crowley promptly sat in the empty chair. "Ettie, I've something to tell you. Yesterday afternoon, Milton Morcombe agreed to have his mother's body taken for an autopsy. The autopsy was performed last night in a different hospital."

"And?"

"As we suspected, there were several body parts missing."

"I thought as much." Ettie told Crowley how the nurse had ordered an x-ray for her and then assaulted her before getting a phone call.

"You were lucky then; she must have been tipped off by her husband after we left the funeral home. There's a warrant out for the arrest of Deirdre Hadley and her brother. Her brother was the one who signed Judith's death certificate. I've got a warrant to search the Hadleys' home and the funeral parlor. I doubt that we'll find anything since he's had the whole night to destroy any evidence. At least we've got Judith's autopsy report as evidence."

Ettie smiled. "I might be alright to leave this place today."

The detective's lips twitched. "I'd say your job is done and if you're well enough to go home then you should."

"Yes, Maureen said she'd come and look after me, which will make things easier for Elsa-May."

"Maureen seems a good friend to you."

"She's always been a dear friend. The doctor will be making his rounds and I'll tell him I'm fit and well and have someone to look after me at home. I'm pleased this is all over."

"It's not quite over at this stage. Nurse Hadley and her brother are on the run. They could have made quite a sum of money if they've been doing this for a while." Crowley leaned forward. "I'll keep you informed. For now, I'll stay with you until someone arrives."

"No, you help find Nurse Hadley and her brother. Elsa-May or Maureen will be here any minute; I'm sure."

"We've got a team on it. I'm not needed until they're brought in for questioning." He pulled his cell phone out of his pocket and studied it.

A moment later, Elsa-May came into the room. When the detective told Elsa-May all that had happened, she insisted Ettie check herself out and not wait for the doctor.

"I'm sure you're alright now, Ettie. We'll book an appointment with your own doctor for this afternoon or tomorrow; he'll give you a general check-up. I find it too eerie for you to stay in this place any longer than necessary."

Ettie looked at the detective and he nodded. "It's most likely best that you go home, Ettie. That is, if you feel up to it."

"I felt up to it days ago."

When the detective left, Elsa-May set about packing the small bag that Ettie brought to the hospital.

"Elsa-May, I told the detective that you or Maureen would be in soon and he insisted on waiting. I thought that I saw in his eyes that he was disappointed that Maureen hadn't come by this morning."

"Why would she come in this early?"

"You're missing my point, Elsa-May. Do you think it's possible that the detective is sweet on Maureen?"

Elsa-May looked up from folding Ettie's nightgown. She studied Ettie for a moment before she said, "*Nee,* I don't think so. And you should not think about such things either. Do not mention anything of the kind to Maureen."

Ettie frowned and wondered why it was that Elsa-May never agreed with anything she suggested.

Nurse McBride breezed into the room. "Morning."

"Good morning," Ettie said, then leaned over and asked Elsa-May to make her a cup of tea.

When Elsa-May left the room, the nurse looked at Ettie's half packed bag. "Are you going home today?"

"Yes, I'm feeling better and I'll get my own doctor to look at me this afternoon. I'm sure I'll feel even better in my own home."

The nurse looked over her shoulder at the door then turned back to Ettie. "There are rumors going around the hospital about Nurse Hadley being arrested. Did your policeman friend have anything to do with that?"

"Yes, and the information you gave me was very helpful. Thank you."

The nurse smiled while she took Ettie's blood pressure.

"My policeman friend said Deirdre's husband has been arrested too. It was something to do with selling body organs."

"That's terrible," nurse McBride said.

"My friend also said that there was a warrant out for the arrest of nurse Hadley's brother."

"I always thought that there was something funny about both of them."

"And you were right," Ettie said. "The police also think there is someone else involved here in the hospital."

"Really? Why, what did they say?"

"That's all my friend told me."

Nurse McBride stepped back from Ettie. "I can't imagine anyone else here would be involved in something like that."

Ettie shrugged her shoulders just as Elsa-May came back in the room with her tea. The nurse left the room after she took Ettie's temperature and jotted some figures on Ettie's chart.

Elsa-May frowned. "I don't know why you want more tea. You've had three cups this morning already. You know the doctor told you less tea and more water."

"I just wanted a word alone with nurse McBride. Something is not right; I can feel it in my bones."

"Do you think that she's involved somehow?"

"*Jah*, but I don't know how she's involved," Ettie scratched her chin.

"What should we do? How will we find out?"

"Follow her see, what she does," Ettie said.

Elsa-May raised her eyebrows at her *schweschder's* order then promptly hurried out of the room.

124

While Elsa-May was gone, Ettie prayed they would get to the bottom of the goings on at the hospital.

Five minutes later, a breathless Elsa-May arrived back to Ettie's room.

"Well?" Ettie asked.

"She was on her cell phone. I saw her in one of the staff rooms and she looked worried as she spoke. I waited, and when she finished speaking she carried on with her duties."

"Is that all?"

When Elsa-May nodded, Ettie tapped her finger on her cheek. "Who would she have called; an accomplice?"

"Accomplice to what though, Ettie?"

"To what's been going on. Let's figure this thing out with logic. Why would she take the opportunity to spread rumors about Hadley yet neglect to tell me that Hadley had recently married a funeral director? She told me just a piece of what she knew."

"Do you still call it a rumor if it's true?" Elsa-

May asked.

Ettie sighed. "Hush, it's an effort for me to speak too much."

Elsa-May nodded. "Could she have wanted nurse Hadley to get into some kind of trouble, but not her new husband and maybe not Hadley's *bruder*?" Elsa-May asked.

Ettie shook her head. "*Nee*, that would not make sense. If nurse Hadley got found out so would all those associated with her."

"Well then, maybe she knew that someone would find them all out, and she wasn't protecting anyone, she was simply pretending not to know too much." Elsa-May suggested.

"Why hadn't she made a complaint? Crowley said anyone can make a complaint and the hospital would not have been told it was she who lodged it. *Nee*, there's something more to that girl; I don't know why I didn't see that in the first place."

"Do you think she was the one who gave the injection to Judith? What if she's the one and not nurse Hadley?"

"*Nee*. I overheard someone on Deirdre's cell telling her to leave the hospital. They wouldn't tell her to leave if she were innocent." Ettie realized that she had forgotten to tell Elsa-May about her encounter with nurse Hadley in the x-ray room, so she filled her in.

"You should have told me sooner, Ettie."

"*Ach, jah*. I forgot." Ettie put her fingers to her mouth. "What if nurse McBride is doing it too? What if she was simply ridding the hospital of her competition?"

"That does make sense, but it does sound extreme that two lots of people can be doing the same thing in the one hospital. What do we do; how do we find out?" Elsa-May asked.

Ettie lay back into her pillows. "I'm a little tired. Can you call Crowley and give him Melanie McBride's name and see what he can dig up?"

Elsa-May patted Ettie on her shoulder. "You relax now. I'll call him." Elsa-May picked up the receiver of the telephone next to Ettie's bed and spoke to detective Crowley.

After Elsa-May called Crowley, she packed the rest of Ettie's belongings and called a taxi to take them home.

Chapter 12

While the earth remaineth, seedtime and harvest,
and cold and heat, and summer and winter,
and day and night shall not cease.
Genesis 8:22

That night, the widows all heard the news that Ettie was home. Ettie was tucked up with a blanket, on a new couch in the living room when Maureen, Emma and Silvie came through her door.

"Tell us what happened, Ettie," Emma said.

"I'll let Elsa-May speak," Ettie said, preferring to conserve her energy.

Everyone turned to Elsa-May.

"Detective Crowley told me this afternoon that they arrested Deirdre Hadley at the airport just as she was about to fly out of the country. Minutes later, they arrested her *bruder* who was booked on a different flight." Elsa-May turned to Emma and explained, "Deirdre's brother was a doctor in the hospital and he was involved as well."

Seeing Emma and Silvie's confused faces Maureen explained, "You see, this is the way that Crowley told me; the nurse gave an injection to paralyze the people; her *bruder,* the doctor, signed the death certificates saying they were dead, but they might not have been. The body parts were removed at the funeral home where they had an operating room."

Silvie asked, "How would they ensure that the bodies went to Mr. Hadley's funeral home?"

"Seems a great many of them did since it's the biggest and the most economical in the area," Elsa-May said. "When they got the body parts they were flown to whoever had paid the highest price."

"Crowley said that in Singapore a kidney is illegally sold for as much as $600,000," Maureen added.

"He also told me," Elsa-May said, "that the nurse and her brother admitted to their crimes. I think they were trying to justify their crime by only using people who were over fifty because they'd already lived a good life. Since Deirdre's brother worked in the emergency room, he picked the likely candidates and Deirdre gave them the injection and the process started from there."

Silvie asked, "Wouldn't it be better to use younger peoples' organs?"

"Since the nurse's husband owned a funeral home wouldn't they have had access to many bodies? Why not just wait until a body came in from somewhere else? Why pick these particular people from the hospital?" Emma asked.

Ettie whispered, "Emma, they wanted their organs fresh."

"Oooh." Emma pulled a face.

Elsa-May looked up from her knitting and said, "I asked the very same thing of Crowley this afternoon, Emma. He said it was quite likely they would not have disclosed the age of the donors to the recipients. If they could do what they did then telling some lies would not concern them."

Emma reached over and grabbed Ettie's hand. "Ettie, how clever of you to notice the nurse giving Judith the injection. If you hadn't been there and seen that, there's no telling how long it would have carried on."

"I knew Judith wasn't supposed to get an injection; they'd only given her pills. At first I thought I'd had a dream and then I realized that I wasn't dreaming at all. It was real."

Elsa-May said, "It was good that Maureen overheard what she did too."

Maureen nodded as she remembered the overheard conversation of the nurses who were giggling about the fact that Nurse Hadley had just married a funeral director.

After Emma let go of Ettie's hand, she dropped her hand by the side of the couch to stroke her dog Ginger. Ginger had not left Ettie's side since she had come home from the hospital. "It was the nurse in the hospital who's really due the credit. She gave me the names of people who died suddenly when they weren't supposed to; she gave me Deirdre's name as well. If it weren't for her then Crowley would have had nothing to work with."

There was a knock on the door. Being in the

middle of her row of knitting, Elsa-May placed the knitting carefully on the chair she'd been sitting on before she opened the door. "Detective Crowley, right on time."

"Good evening, ladies. I thought you might all be here," he said as he walked into Ettie and Elsa-May's small living room.

"Have a seat," Elsa-May said.

He sat down on one of the chairs. "Ettie, you're on a couch. I've never seen a couch here before, just these chairs." He hit the side of the old wooden chair.

"Bailey gave it to us. It was here when I got back from the hospital." Ettie smiled as she nestled further into the two pillows behind her back.

"Bailey knew that Ettie would not want to stay in bed all the day long. She needs rest. He thought the couch would enable her to rest out of her bedroom," Elsa-May explained.

Ettie knew that the doctor told her to walk around, but was glad Elsa-May had forgotten that piece of doctor's advice. Ettie would much rather rest than walk.

"You ladies all know what happened?" Crowley looked at each of the five widows in turn. "How we've arrested the three main people involved?"

"So they're all arrested now?" Emma asked.

Crowley nodded and said, "I'm going to the hospital tomorrow to see if anyone is prepared to come forward and give evidence. We need as many people as we can to testify." Crowley laughed.

"You rarely laugh, Detective. What do you find so funny?" Silvie asked.

"It's hard for me to believe that a major operation of this kind has been busted by a hunch from an Amish widow and overheard conversations." He turned to Maureen. "I especially want to thank you, Maureen. If you hadn't come with me to speak to Mr. Morcombe he might never have given his consent to collect his mother's body. Then, I would have had nothing. I certainly had no evidence to obtain a warrant before that."

Maureen smiled. "I'm glad I could help. I don't like the thought of people having to die before their time. At the same time, it is awful that there aren't enough organs available for transplant for those who need them."

Ettie put a finger in the air to gain Crowley's attention. "What of the nurse; nurse McBride? Did you find out anything about her, Detective?"

Crowley turned to Elsa-May. "Do you want to tell her, or shall I?"

Elsa-May looked up from her knitting and began, "When you were asleep this afternoon, Ettie, I went back to the hospital and asked some questions." Elsa-May gave a chortle. "You're not the only one who can persuade people to tell you things."

"You asked questions about Melanie McBride?" Ettie asked.

"*Jah* it seems not all of the people who died suspiciously did so on the 8 p.m. to 3 a.m. shift."

Ettie opened her mouth in shock. "What? I naturally believed what Melanie told me. I never thought that she would have reason to lie about things. She pointed us specifically in Deirdre

Hadley's direction."

Elsa-May said, "It seems that Hadley took over Melanie's business when she married the funeral director and Melanie was annoyed; that's when Melanie started rumors in the hospital about Deirdre Hadley."

Ettie's brow furrowed. "Well how could you possibly know that for sure? No one at the hospital would have told you such a thing. They would be in terrible trouble if they knew so much and kept quiet."

"Quite right, Ettie," Crowley said. "When Elsa-May gave me McBride's name, I checked with the Department of Health and there were complaints against her. Because they were personal complaints, they had not come up in my search of general complaints against the hospital. In the past year alone, Melanie McBride has been investigated twice by the Department of Health. They were not able to find anything conclusive against her."

"Until..." Elsa-May said.

"Until what?" Ettie turned her head to hear what

Elsa-May had to say.

Crowley took over, "No one had any solid evidence against her until Deirdre gave us a full written account of what she knew of her activities."

Ettie leaned back into her pillows and breathed out heavily. "I was right; Melanie McBride was involved in something. I didn't think so at first, but as the days went on, something did not sit right with me."

Crowley cleared his throat. "Deirdre was quite pleased to give as much information as she could on Melanie." Crowley chuckled. "Most likely thinking that she would get a reduced sentence. There's a warrant out now for McBride's arrest."

"Melanie seemed so sweet," Ettie said while stroking her dog. "Why did you wait for so long to tell me all this, Elsa-May?"

Elsa-May exchanged a knowing look with Crowley. "Detective Crowley wanted me to wait until he got here to tell you about Melanie McBride."

Emma stood. "You'll stay for cake and tea,

Detective?"

A seldom seen smile spread across Crowley's face. "Yes, of course."

And we know that all things work together for good to them that love God, to them who are the called according to his purpose.
Romans 8:28

* * * The End * * *
* * * * * * * * * * * * * *

138

Watch for Book 10 in the '*Amish Secret Widows' Society'* series.

One of Ettie's estranged daughters, Myra, turns up unexpectedly on Ettie's doorstep. Myra who ran away from the Amish as a teen, tells Ettie that her *Englischer* husband of ten years, Hunter Wallace, has disappeared without a trace. When Myra went to file a missing person's report she found that the person she knew as Hunter Wallace does not exist. The widows agree to help Ettie's daughter and enlist the assistance of Detective Crowley. As if trying to stop them from making enquiries, strange accidents beset the widows. Who is behind Hunter's disappearance and why is there no record of his birth? Will the widows be able to solve the Hunter Wallace mystery before one of them gets hurt, or worse?

Other books in the
'Amish Secret Widows' Society':

<u>The Amish Widow: Book 1</u>

Newly widowed Amish woman Emma Kurtzler has little time to grieve before she discovers that someone is trying to force her from her farm.

The man who had the lease on her farm is found murdered shortly after informing Emma of his intention to break the lease.

In an effort to both save her farm and avoid becoming a suspect in the man's murder, Emma sets out to get to the bottom of things.

Emma befriends a group of Amish Widows and quickly discovers that there is more to these sweet Amish ladies than meets the eye when they willingly help her with her investigations.

In the midst of Emma's troubles she is drawn to Wil Jacobson, a friendly neighbor, but can she trust this man who is trying his best to win her heart?

Hidden: Book 2

It's another murder to solve for the Amish Secret Widows' Society.

An elderly Amish man, rumored to be in the possession of paintings worth millions of dollars, is found poisoned.

Can the widows find out who killed him before there is another murder?

Emma Kurtzler is in love with Wil Jacobson but struggles with it being too soon to marry after the death of her husband.

Meanwhile, Silvie Keim is swept off her feet by Bailey Abler. Bailey is a mysterious stranger who is staying within the community and proclaims he wants to be Amish.

What connection does Bailey have to the murdered man that will shock the community?

What will Silvie do when she discovers Bailey's true identity?

<u>Accused: Book 3</u>

Meet all the widows again as they endeavor to solve another murder. This time the murder took place some years ago.

On her aunt's insistence, Amish woman Angela Bontreger has been writing to Robert Geiger. When Angela travels from her small town to meet Robert in person, he denies knowledge of her and the letters.

As they talk further, Robert tells Angela that his late brother was accused of murder. Angela's aunt Elsa-May and the other widows offer to help Robert clear his brother's name.

Will Robert see past the tragedies that have plagued his life to realize that he is falling in love with Angela?

Will Angela go home to her small town without the love of the man she wants?

<u>Amish Regrets: Book 4</u>

There is another mystery for the widows to solve. This time there is a murder close to home. Silvie's younger sister, Sabrina, has become involved with the millionaire *Englischer*, Carmello Liante.

When Carmello is found murdered and Sabrina becomes a suspect, the widows rally around to find the killer.

In their investigations, they find many people who wanted to see Carmello dead. Even more suspects come to the fore once the benefactors of Carmello's will are made known.

In the midst of her grieving Sabrina must decide whether to stay in the Amish community.

Will Sabrina accept what the bishop proposes she should do to make amends?

Or will the grieving Sabrina decide to leave the community for good now that her shameful secret is out.

Amish House of Secrets: Book 5

Wil buys an old house to renovate for Emma and he to live in after they are married.

What does Emma find in the old house that sends her on a journey to unite lost loves?

Join the five widows as they endeavor to reunite two people who have been kept apart for over forty years through lies and deceit.

While Emma is trying to repair another's relationship, is she at risk of letting her own happiness fall by the wayside?

Emma takes advice from others regarding her relationship, but when she realizes her true feelings has she left things too late?

Amish Undercover: Book 6

In best selling Amish fiction author Samantha Price's new-release, the five Amish widows have another mystery to solve.

FBI agent, Bailey Rivers, has thought long and hard about his life.

He has spoken to the bishop and is set to join the Amish community and leave the English world behind.

His decision was made easy by his love for the Amish widow, Silvie Kiem.

Silvie persuades the other widows to help Bailey

solve his last case, the case he has worked on for years.

The widows come up with an elaborate plan, and Emma, despite Bailey's warnings, goes undercover in an effort to obtain information on stolen paintings.

Will the widows' efforts turn out to be far more dangerous than any of them anticipated?

Will Bailey be able to join the Amish community and marry the woman he loves not knowing whether he can close the case that he has been working on for years?

Amish Breaking Point: Book 7

With his wedding only weeks away, the newly Amish Bailey Rivers is desperate to uncover the terrifying secret that lies buried deep within his mind.

Bailey keeps his problem from his bride-to-be, Silvie, and enlists the help of the other widows to put the pieces of his past together.

Bailey is determined to get to the bottom of the

flashes of terrifying memories that haunt his nights.

And why will no one tell him the true reason that his grandfather left the Amish so many years ago?

When Bailey finally discovers the truth, will it be so troubling that he will wish that he had left things well alone?

Will he ever be able to bury his past and move ahead with the woman he loves?

Plain Murder: Book 8

When Silvie visits her sister, Sabrina, at the stables where she works, she stumbles across a dead body. Sabrina's boss, Mr. Caruthers, has been murdered. Trevor, the boss's son, becomes one of the many suspects, and is arrested.

Mr. Caruthers' other son, the handsome Jamie Caruthers, steps in to run the business. This upsets John Steele, the stable manager.

Bailey, ex-FBI agent and Sabrina's brother-in-law, is roped in to helping Detective

, but does it prove too much too soon, given his recent breakdown?

Sabrina knows that Trevor and his father never saw eye to eye, but she doubts Trevor killed his father.

Sabrina seeks help from her widow friends to discover who really killed her boss, Mr. Caruthers.

****

Other **#1 BEST SELLING** series
by Samantha Price
'Amish Twin Hearts' series:

****

Also a **#1 BEST-SELLING** series-

'Amish Wedding Season' series
by Samantha Price:

****

Books in the **#1 BEST SELLING**
*'**Amish Romance Secrets**'* series
by Samantha Price:

A Simple Choice: Book 1

When Kate was 14, the 19 year old Benjamin promised to marry her when she was old enough.

Yet a few years later, Kate finds that Benjamin has married another Amish woman. Why did the honorable Benjamin go back on his word and marry someone else?

Kate's faith is shaken, and she vows to leave

the Amish as soon as she is able.

After four years living in the *Englisch* world, Kate feels neither Amish nor *Englisch*.

To make matters worse, living away from the community and away from Benjamin has done nothing to lessen Kate's feelings for him.

Kate asks God to grant her a husband, yet never in her wildest dreams could she have imagined the way in which this unfolds.

Annie's Faith: Book 2

Annie is determined to win the handsome Jessie Yoder's heart.

The only thing standing in Annie's way is Liz, a long-term house guest of Annie's family.

Annie is downcast as Jessie cannot take his eyes off Liz.

Liz is everything that Annie is not.

While Annie wears plain clothes and no makeup, Liz wears the latest English fashions and is never seen without makeup or high heels.

Things go from bad to worse when Liz appears

to be returning Jessie's attentions.

How can Annie possibly compete with the beautiful Liz to win Jessie's heart while staying true to her Amish values?

A Small Secret: Book 3

When Sarah falls in love with John, an *Englisher,* she is momentarily drawn away from her faith. When Sarah discovers she is having John's child, she attempts to hide her shame from the community.

John professes his love for Sarah through his letters, but when he doesn't send for her as promised, Sarah decides to keep the baby a secret from him.

She sets out to make a life for herself and her baby.

Sarah finds out first hand about God's forgiveness as she sees her life transform in a way she never thought possible.

Ephraim's Chance: Book 4

Ephraim has fallen in love with Liz. However, Ephraim's mother has other ideas and sets about for him to marry Ruth, a good Amish girl.

Liz is heartbroken and fears that not even returning to the Amish will be enough to win Ephraim's mother's approval. Ephraim decides to go against his controlling mother's wishes, but has he left things too late?

Ephraim discovers that Liz is being pursued by a handsome, rich doctor. Ephraim fears that even if he is successful in his bid to win Liz, his secret may be enough to lose her forever.

A Second Chance: Book 5

True love does not strike twice in one lifetime - that is what fifty-three year old Rebecca thought until she met the Amish man, Jeremiah.

While Rebecca contemplates her baptism and return to the Amish, her late husband's niece, Morgan, lands on her doorstep.

Rebecca tries to help the troubled teenager sort

out her problems, but Jeremiah has very different ideas about how this should be achieved.

Will the relentless aggravation of this rebellious teen and the constant reminder of the intense love that Rebecca had for her late husband be enough to drive away Jeremiah?

Will Rebecca's desire to help her niece lose her a second chance at love?

Choosing Amish: Book 6

Morgan, a tattooed girl with a past, and Amish man, Jacob, have fallen in love. Having been caught up in a whirlwind romance, neither one of them has faced what is now standing between them.

One of them must choose to leave their past life behind them in order to create a life together.

Knowing that Jacob's sisters have found out about her past Morgan wonders if she will ever be accepted by Jacob's family.

Will Jacob leave the only life he has ever known as well as his faith for an uncertain future in the English world to be with Morgan?

Short Stories by Samantha Price:
'Single Amish Romance Short Stories'
series by Samantha Price:

Connect with Samantha Price at:
samanthaprice333@gmail.com
http//twitter.com/AmishRomance

31052878R00089

Made in the USA
San Bernardino, CA
29 February 2016